48

wn~

you get to come again!

Meli Camille Calha

MONTEZUMA
RED

CAMILLE CALHOUN

MONTEZUMA RED

iUniverse books may be ordered through booksellers or by contacting:

iUniverse
1663 Liberty Drive
Bloomington, IN 47403
www.iuniverse.com
1-800-Authors (1-800-288-4677)

ISBN: 978-1-5320-3494-7 (sc)
ISBN: 978-1-5320-3493-0 (e)

Library of Congress Control Number: 2017917198

Print information available on the last page.

iUniverse rev. date: 11/29/2017

I would like to thank God first and foremost for everything! I would also like to thank my awesome husband who has always been supportive and encouraging. I want to thank my son, Josh, for designing "Effie" for the front cover and his sweet wife Emmie for reading it. Thanks to my mom who was the first to proof-read the manuscript.

PROLOGUE

January, 2011

There she is looking at me again. Those dull, green, tired eyes staring at me, noticing the new lines around my eyes I'm sure! Such a discriminating glare, so much judgment as they roam over my hair and face. Who does she think she is to look at me so? As if she knows every thought, every secret and reason for keeping them. Well, I see her too. She's a complete fraud! And if it weren't for those monthly trips to the beauty salon she most definitely would not have that chestnut brown hair. She doesn't look like she used to either. She doesn't act like she used to, she tells the truth now. At least most of the time.

And so, goes my regular morning conversation as I stare at myself in this too clean mirror that reflects so much more than what is sitting in front of it. I sit in my little lovely room at my own personal antique dresser (they allow us to bring our own furniture here) and carefully apply my make-up. This process takes a little longer than it used to, partly because I'm not in a rush to go to work, and partly because if I don't steady my hand I will end up looking like the "Joker" from my great-grandson's movie "Batman". Pam will be in shortly to help me put my still fairly thick hair in my favorite up-do. So, it is true…I am still vain. I believe as I have always believed…..no, let me say that ever since Lucy instilled in me her philosophy of beauty, that one should always look their best. To give the world something pleasant to look at. There was always one who said I was "sure something to look at!" I gazed down to my dresser and let my eyes linger on the face and body that was now confined to a five by seven world. My husband…my own personal guardian angel, teacher, friend…if anyone could hear my thoughts they would think I was exaggerating my view of him since he was no longer with me. That is not the case. He was just as I believed him to be. Before my mind begins to wander too far down that path, Pam, my sweet young nursing assistant comes in to help me. We have several different assistants, but Pam is always so upbeat and positive even though taking care of us can hardly be called a glamorous job.

"Good morning Ms. Effie! How you doin' this morning? Don't you look so nice today! What a pretty color you have on!" Beams Pam in her usual way.

"Oh, you are being kind Pam, how do you always manage to be so…. peppy in the mornings?"

"Three cups of coffee and getting to see my favorite resident!" she says with honest to goodness compassion in her face as she begins the morning routine of coiffing my hair just like I like it.

"Well, I'm sure the coffee is the greater of the two. But I'm grateful to you just the same. And I'm grateful that you take such pains to help me look presentable."

"Ms. Effie, you look as sassy as you did in those pictures. She nods toward the small shrine on my dressing table. "How old were you in this one? Was that one before you got married?" She fired questions too rapidly to answer each one at a time. "I was eighteen in that one. Just before the war hit my area so hard. And that one was when I was several years older, but yes I was already married." I answered as casually as I could. All these years later and I still mourn for that young girl. Pam isn't quite finished with her seemingly harmless interrogation. "Those pictures of you and your kids are great, you look like you were having a ball in that one." Pam motions to one of my many family vacation pictures with the tip of my comb. "Where were you all?" I let my eyes linger on the 5x7 memory of my husband and two children waving and pointing behind them to Niagara Falls. "That was one of our trips to Niagara Falls." My sweet husband and my children. My son, Jon, with his wide-open smile, always happy, always optimistic. My Ruthie, a half-smile, trying so hard to appear to be getting too old to enjoy these trips, but really did. My heart always felt such contradiction within itself when I looked at my pictures of my children. It has been so full of love and regret at the same time, from the first time I laid my eyes on each of their newborn faces.

"Did you hear me Miss Effie? Up or down today?" Oh, thank you Pam for dragging me back before I lingered too long. "Up I think. Dierk always liked it up." I said with a quick glance back down to his picture.

"I especially like the one of you in front of your store. You were just a go-getter weren't you? What *were* you like back then Miss Effie? A wife, a mother, a business owner.… I bet you've got some stories to tell!"

Well, she certainly didn't know she just made the understatement of the century. "I am sorry to stifle your romantic notions, but I'm afraid there's just not much to tell. I was married, I worked, raised my children, and now I'm here." I say with as much conviction as a prisoner begging to stay behind bars.

"Mmmhhm.… yeah, somehow, I don't believe that. How about that handsome husband of yours? Did you meet during the war?"

"Well, now, that's a story indeed. Yes…yes we did meet during the war." My smile faded slightly and my heart felt that same dull heaviness as I thought about my husband, the war, and my children.

"A war-time bride…that's so romantic Ms. Effie!" Pam continues to gently pry as she brushes and twists and pins.

I lifted my eyes to meet her gaze in the mirror. Romantic? No, not by the standards that dictate the nostalgic novels of today. Necessary? Life-saving? Absolutely, one-hundred percent both. My own children didn't even know all the details of how my husband and I met. I almost feel compelled to test the waters so to speak and see what horrifying reaction I might get. But what if she doesn't think I'm terrible? What if she sees the pain and struggles behind all of my decisions? If this person, this acquaintance, could see the good of what I did, what we all did, maybe, just maybe my children could too. Taking a deep breath, maybe out of life-long fatigue, maybe a deep breath to hold while I plunge into the deep end, I'm not sure, but plunge I did.

"I suppose I could tell you why I always wear my red lipstick…"

CHAPTER ONE

June 1939
Wiesbaden, Germany 1939

I was seventeen in 1939. I had just finished school as had all my closest girlfriends. Oh, we were the queens of the universe, young, beautiful, invincible, and certainly we must have been the most desirable young ladies that had celebrated their coming out. We were a fiery group, each one of us completely individual yet completely complimentary, making us a force to be reckoned with…. or so we believed.

Anneliese Strauss and I had been best friends literally from birth, our parents having been neighbors and expecting at nearly the same time. Anneliese was vocal when I was quiet, daring when I was cautious, and flirtatious when I was shy. So, you see, I needed her to be able to live outside myself, and she needed me to keep her from flying off the face of the earth.

Brigitte Faust was our link to the super-intellectual world. She was also our guarantee for graduation. We were all smart and talented, but she had that extra "depth" of intelligence. She came complete with unmovable ideals of not marrying, becoming a nurse or more likely a doctor, and literally saving the world, or if her science "experiments" were any indication of her future,…destroying it.

And then there was me. How do I describe myself as a 17-year-old to you? I was eager to begin the next phase of my life, maybe not the life my parents had planned, but an adventure of sorts, a way to re-create myself out from under Anneliese's popular shadow…using my own intellect and wit instead of depending on Brigitte. I had those qualities; I had a streak of spontaneity, a slightly rebellious spark and enough wits about me that surely, I could make *some* of my own decisions. I had been referred to as the attractive one of us, and maybe I was, but there had to be more to me than the external. Don't mistake my ambitions to mean that I wanted to break away from my closest friends; on the contrary, I just wanted to be a stronger contributor to our group.

But isn't that the usual way of it? Three close friends, all different, all female stereotypes accounted for? And so, we were; three points of a triangle, each looking out to a different space to gravitate toward, yet knowing without the other leg or apex we would surely lose our complete identity of "our group".

There were others that hovered around the perimeter of our group. The "male" others that had their sights set on matrimony or rather the physical reward of matrimony. Anneliese thoroughly enjoyed toying with the three regulars that would pal around with us. She had a way of making each one believe she spent sleepless nights thinking only of them; truth being she didn't think of any of them more than a break in the monotony. Of course, they were guaranteed dates to cotillions and other coming out parties or a movie, so their worth was such that we didn't want to completely run them off, but certainly didn't want to be over-encouraging.

My parents were especially fond of Armin Mueller. Good family, good connections, a "nice up-and-coming" German youth. How was *he* supposed to help me re-create myself? No, he was nice enough company, but definitely not the means to my desired end.

Then there was Axel Walchter and Joseph (Sepp) Lutz. We always teased Brigitte that she would one day disappoint the world and it's need for her brilliance by marrying Axel. This, of course, would put her in such a foul mood it was all she could do to force a smile on her face and maintain polite conversation with the poor young man. Here she would be steaming and he would be looking at her with the biggest cow eyes I have ever seen. As far as Sepp, I have to say I didn't really know him that well. He had moved to Wiesbaden from Munich and was really rather quiet, back then. I have since come to know him better.

And so, it went through the summer of 1939. All of us enjoying our youth, the gatherings, the flirting, the feeling of greatly anticipating that next great step or leap or plunge or whichever mode of transport we chose to transition from past to future. What a breathless whirlwind of a time it was, dressing up, putting on make-up and borrowing this dress or that scarf, dabbing on a bit of Mama's perfume then going dancing or walking and laughing and just maybe allowing that stolen kiss now and again. How could we have known, how could anyone in our age group have known what was coming; what September 1st was going to usher into the world and what it would rip from it?

Lakeside Assisted Living
February, 2011

As I sit in the sun-room at the front of the assisted living allowing my limbs to soak in the Godly version of vitamin D, I find myself thinking more and more about those days. Days that I thought were well placed in a lavender scented box tied up in tissue paper. My kids were only vaguely aware of the heirloom of my memories and regrets. I have longed to tell them many times over the years, but it never seemed right. It never seemed appropriate timing or beneficial for them to know. The time is coming that I will have to tell them, I wish I had while their father was still alive. Now, our relationships are so different. Jon has always been such a calm, positive, silver-lining kind of person, I think he would come closer to understanding my choices than Ruth. Ruth is very independent, slightly more pessimistic, and very much like me. And, much like myself, she will be much less likely to forgive me. I can't say what is prompting me to tell my young friend or how much I will tell her. Maybe I'm just wanting someone to hear it, to tell me it's going to be ok when I do tell the kids. Even as I'm thinking this, something in me knows whether I tell all to Pam or not, my children should be the ones to hear it. I can almost hear Ruth if she knew I had told a mere acquaintance all of my well-hidden secrets and not her. "Really mother! You once again felt selfish enough to do things your way! You just had to blab your life story to a stranger instead of us!" Yes, that is most assuredly what she would say, and she would be right. I also know that as I'm thinking of rehearsing my story to Pam, I know that I will not tell her *all* of it, after all what will she think of me? Will she understand the time we had to survive? Does it matter? Never the less I have already started telling Pam about my childhood and will continue sharing some of my memories with her but the real truth of it is I'm building enough nerve to tell my children the whole truth. So, young Pam and I begin a ritual of daily waltzing down my own memory lane. Sometimes we talk while she helps me get ready, sometimes I share a funny story as she walks with me to the dining room. She thinks it was such a romantic time to have lived and in some respects, it was. Youth and new beginnings and all sorts of "firsts" are always romantic. She loves to hear about the way we dressed, the way we looked, the way we danced... she referred to all of these as being so lady-like. She says it's very different than the way young people behave today and certainly different from their dating rituals of today. I just smile when she says those things. Hair styles, dress, make-up, even dances change...but not everything changes. She seems to believe every girl during that time was as pure as the driven snow. The thing about telling someone stories of your past is, they don't have a choice but to believe the story the way it's told. A slight change of one aspect or another and the speaker can create just the history they want the audience to believe. I keep my stories light, it's more fun that way. I like seeing her eyes light up with laughter or wonder. I could easily spin this tale to make myself the heroine, not the horrible.

February, 1940

Everything was changing so fast in each of our lives. The question of the day was not which party to attend, but which party to join as if there were a choice. Armin, Axel, and Sepp were of course called on to serve in the Schutzstaffel or SS. Due to not only their educational background, financial positions of their families, but they were "true" Germans. There were no traces of Jewish people in their histories. And because they were known as true loyalists to Germany and found to be "obedient" to country, they were obvious choices to be in the elitist group. The last I had heard; Axel and Sepp were a part of the Waffen-SS and Armin was a part of the Allgemeine-SS. These were terms completely new to me, and showing my young age, I didn't think much about finding out more. Brigitte was doing her part by joining the German Red Cross as a helferin (helper nurse). There weren't as many uses for German women in the military, maybe some clerical and she felt she could do the best with the Red Cross. Brigitte was an absolute loyalist to Germany and wanted nothing more than to be found serving the Fuehrer 100 percent. Besides, this was lining right up with her desire to be a nurse. As far back as I can remember, Brigette was wrapping bandages on dolls, her brothers, and even us when we would let her. She could be such a strong bossy sort that we usually acquiesced to whatever ailment she was trying to cure in us. She always excelled in sciences and often tried to create her own experiments outside of the classroom. I'm sure she was just as much of a fire ball as she was back then while she was learning to be a nurse.

Anneliese had found herself being more confined to her mother's house to care for her. Her mother's health had rapidly declined in the latter half of 1939. I visited when I could, but Father preferred I stayed close to home now. When I was able to visit, I was often in awe of how mature Anne had become during this trying time. As I would watch her care for her mother with strength and patience I would wonder where those characteristics had been hiding all those years. She was a kind person of course, but definitely more interested in the superficial. Now she barely fixed her hair other than a quick brush through and a bun. She seemed to have replaced all frivolous routines with bathing her mom, keeping her turned and comfortable, feeding her…funny how life events mold us and pull out the best or worst of our character.

And as for me…. I was in a stupor. What was I supposed to be doing? I had never been one to be extremely involved in the political realm of our country, but when war comes, it's no longer just the political realm, its public and it's private. It's secular and it's religious. It's far and it's near. Is it one's responsibility to their country to blindly follow? I did not understand at the time the motive behind Hitler's aggressive war, but just the fact that so many were blindly following was beyond unsettling to me. But I was still a German. This was my country, my home. The question that fluttered around in my mind was who is truly trying to take my home and change my country? Is it the "Polish sector of criminals"? Is it the "dishonest Jew"? I didn't know before that we were supposed to think of our friends and acquaintances that way. I didn't know that the dear man and his wife that owned the local jewelry store were really supposed to be the enemy. Well, thankful to German propaganda, we were well informed. The trouble with that was I couldn't bring myself to believe it. There, I said it; I was already traitorous in my heart long before my actions became so. I would have never dared to speak my thoughts, especially not to my friends. We were all raised in the same neighborhood, we had always attended the same schools, social functions. We shared clothes, make-up, secret crushes… but we didn't share my questions, my wonderings of the chaos that was becoming more prevalent and closer to home. I didn't share any thoughts that ran deeper than the superficial thoughts of a teenager with my parents and as an only child, well that just left my friends. Somehow, I just couldn't bring myself to say, "isn't this madness? Do we really consider our long-time neighbors our enemies?" But as fate would have it the opportunity to even speak to my friends was becoming more and more rare. My days began to take on an automated lonely type of existence. I helped Mother with whatever household project she had in the works, went with her to the church, to the market, tended the small garden. I couldn't remember a time that I had not been with or spoke to my friends almost daily. It felt as if they had been allowed to cross the threshold of adulthood, while I carried on the same as I always had. I felt lonely, left out and very much like a baby. I was jealous that Brigette took the reins of her own life and was full steam ahead and as crazy as it sounded, I was even jealous of the now reversed relationship between Anne and her mother. Not that I would ever wish illness on anyone especially not my mother, I just couldn't understand why life was continuing on for my friends and mine had stalled.

CHAPTER TWO

MAY 1940

It had been months since I had been able to speak with Brigitte. I heard that she was to be stationed at a place about 90 miles north of Berlin called Ravensbruck. I was sure she was utilizing her nursing skills as part of the Aufseherin. I was quite certain that she was doing her part for Germany, whether it was using her sought after nursing skills or cooking or sewing; whatever needed to be done. This was how we were all raised. We were raised to work hard, to contribute to our German community, and to be prouder of the craftsmanship and products that we produced than the money to be made from them. One must understand what we had been taught not only in school but in our homes and in our society as well. From as early as the fourth grade through the eighth grade many were taught as German children about the purity of our race versus the impurity of the Jewish race, for they were taught they were a separate race, not a religion. It was taught that the Jew subjugated other races by controlling their money as bankers and lenders. The propaganda was taught in school and by some parents and grandparents that the November Revolution of 1918 was a result of the traitorous work of the Jews. Even with all of this, in some places, we as German children were still friends with Jewish children. We were too young to really understand; at least some of us didn't understand. To me, friends were just friends and little Jewish girls that lived here and spoke German just like me *were just like me.* As we grew older it became an unspoken understanding; no German man could take a Jewish girl to be his wife and no German girl could marry a Jewish boy. But to me this still wasn't enough reasoning for some of this hate that seemed to emanate from some German adults and from texts and papers that were printed. So, there we were, German youth, often taught one way and sometimes secretly believing another. I could accept that I wasn't to marry someone Jewish, I had not planned on that anyway. I could accept that they were a different race, not just a different religion. I could even accept that they may be more interested in making loads of money and climbing social ladders and political ones as well. My family had always been well off so what did that matter to me? What I couldn't accept was that according to recent propaganda we were supposed to shun our Jewish friends and acquaintances! In school, we would often just roll our eyes and laugh under our breath when our teachers would spend time trying to convince us of how superior we were. There were too many fun things to think about besides boring political stuff. But now that the war was coming closer and the laws dictating we stay away from the Jews were becoming more enforced, we...I...didn't have a choice but to pay attention. Some groups of Jewish people were being taken to political camps, I assumed it was a holding place until this war ended. The movie reels displayed living quarters that were nice and clean, people were eating well, and in some scenes, were laughing and playing card games. But somehow, I felt something just wasn't right, if they were just eating and sleeping and playing cards, why couldn't they just stay in their homes? Even as gullible as I was, I knew there was more to it than that. This was a prison of some kind...maybe worse. And why were they being separated anyway? We heard the official reports that these people were who were being rounded up were political criminals. Did that include mothers and children? These camps were supposed to house the political criminals and mentally dangerous people. I couldn't believe I was the only person who was astounded that our government actually thought we were all just mindlessly believing everything they were saying. But, what was true? Maybe I needed to find out more for myself. I hated feeling like a rebel, like if my true thoughts were known I'd be the enemy. Maybe I was conjuring up more of a conspiracy than there really was out of my loneliness or boredom. I could remember going for days hanging on all news reports, all conversations between housewives over their picket fences, the late-night conversations between my parents and then becoming distracted by normal teenage girl thoughts. I would long to see my friends and talk about things besides war and camps. I suppose my level of philanthropy had not reached the point of complete consumption.

Anneliese on the other hand was completely consumed with having to take care of her mother and I was sure she could use some help or at least some company. I was so fortunate to still have both of my parents. Anneliese's father left them while she was still in her early teens. Her mother never really recovered from the loss of who she believed to be her soul mate.

Desperate to shake my melancholy and make an attempt at normal conversation; I gathered some tea cookies and tea cakes from our kitchen and wrapped them in a cloth, placed them in my wicker basket that sat firmly between the handle bars of my bicycle and started off to my friends'. I pedaled passed Marktkirche, (Market church), and made my way through the curvy lanes bumping along on cobblestone streets to the apartment on Grabenstrabe. Her mother just wasn't able to keep their home close to us once her father left. My brief ride to her home did little to clear my mind since there were SS officers constantly milling about in our little town.

I pulled my bicycle up to the steps of Anneliese's apartment and carried our treats up to the front door, rang and waited. The Anneliese that opened the door was not the Anneliese that I so wanted to emulate during our younger years. Though her smile seemed to spread from one side of her face to the other, she looked many years older and so very tired. Her hair seemed to be in whatever position it was in when she got out of bed, and I believe this was one of the few times I had ever seen her without make-up. My heart immediately ached for her, but I absolutely refused to let surprise show on my face.

"Oh, Effie! How wonderful to see you!" She reached out to give a warm hug and kiss to my cheek.

"We were spoiled to seeing each other every day in school and now I suppose we have too many grown up things to keep us occupied. I've brought us some treats; do you have time to visit for a little while?" I didn't know how to excuse myself for not coming around more knowing that she had quite a job of taking care of her mother. I had visited from time to time over the past months; by I suppose my immaturity kept me from being any true help.

"Of course! Please come in. Mother has been sleeping most of the day. Let me just look in on her and I will put some tea on." Anneliese directed me to the front room while she quietly looked in on her mother. I could hear her walk to their kitchen and put tea on. As I looked around the apartment I saw pictures of the three of us at some dance. Who were those three girls? Anneliese came in with a tea tray and I began to open our cookies.

"Effie, I'm so sorry we all weren't together for your birthday this year. The 18th birthday is a biggie. Everything has just changed everywhere I guess. Did you at least celebrate well with your parents?" She asked as she poured our tea and gestured toward the cream and a very small bowl of sugar.

"Yes, we did, Mama made a version of my favorite dinner and of course she made her delicious chocolate cake so it was just fine."

"I thought of you on your day, but Mother was so sick, there was no way for me to leave her."

"What do the doctors say now?"

"A matter of time really. The cancer seems to be ravaging her poor little body. I have been told to keep her as comfortable as possible. They have given me something to help with her pain. I wanted to find Father and tell him, but then I decided it may not be for the best."

"Anne, I'm so sorry, is there anything I can do? Is there anything Mama could come do?" What kind of help I was offering I didn't know. I always lived a second or two behind Anne, doing what she did and taking my lead from her.

"No, really, I'm just keeping her comfortable and I really want to be the one with her when it's time." Anne said this with twice the years than was indicated on her birth record.

"I understand, but if you need me, I will be here." We both looked out the window and sipped our tea waiting for the appropriate time to pass to be able to change the subject without seeming calloused.

Anneliese spoke first, "Say, have you heard from Brigitte?"

So much for not dwelling on the thoughts that I was trying to avoid with this visit. "The last I heard she was stationed at Ravensbruck. How about you? Have you heard from any of our friends?"

"I haven't heard from Axel or Sepp directly, but actually Armin has been keeping in touch quite often and he tells me what he has heard."

"Armin, really? I have only heard from him once since they all left." We had all been friends but I had never noticed any special friendship between just the two of them. I guess I had been self-absorbed enough to think he always liked me.

"I know that he was somewhat of a beau for you, does it bother you that he has contacted me? If it does I will of course discourage him." Even as she said this, I could hear the hope that I wouldn't mind, and the strong sense that even if I did, she wouldn't be able to keep the last part of her statement.

"Of course I don't mind! We were really just friends, and you should have someone to talk to. So, how is he? Where is he?"

With a relieved smile Anne replied, "He spends most of his time between Berlin and Munich, but is able to come home every few weeks. He really hasn't told me much about what he does. He just says, 'paper-work, paper-work'."

"Well I am sure that is a nice diversion for both of you to have an old friend to relate to and spend a little time with. He always seemed like a really good guy."

"So, tell me Effie, what is keeping you occupied these days?"

What could I say? I helped Mama at home, helped a little at the church, I thought about the war, my thoughts drifted from the seriousness of the things rumored to be happening to the Jews to the silliness of wishing there were enough guys left in town to date. I thought that I must say something more grown up than that so I decided to do as all adults did, I asked about the war. No getting away from that as a main topic of conversation.

"I have been thinking a lot about the war as everyone is. I feel that I should be doing something. You know, be more proactive like Brigitte. It seems like everyone has moved past school days to actual adulthood and participating in the world around them except me. Does Armin talk about it much when you are together?" I flushed with slight embarrassment as I watched Anne's own complexion pink with a downward glance to her hands. "I mean, of course you have better things to talk about and do when you get to see each other. That was a silly question!"

Anne smiled that half Mona Lisa smile and a shadow of a much older and experienced girl looked back to me. "Well, sure, we try to talk about when we all just hung around, about our friends, family. We...are...really close." If this had been just us talking after a date or a day at school I would have berated her for all the details. And, truthfully, I really wanted to know. I always looked to Anne to live the experiences first, then pass that wisdom on to me. It was hard to think of Armin like that, but seeing the flush on Anne's face let me know there was something more adult, more physical than holding hands on the way home from a movie. Somehow it seemed immature to ask for all the details, everything he said, was he a good kisser, had they gone that far...farther?? Time away from each other since school made that kind of intimate conversation seem very childish. I tuned back in to what she had been saying...obviously not the kind of details to pull me back into the current conversation.

"But it would be strange to not talk about the war...it consumes everyone. Armin says that the fuehrer's leadership will bring jobs and more prosperity. I don't know...I trust what Armin thinks. I don't want to sound selfish, but all I can really think of right now is Mother. One day just flows into another of bathing and feeding and keeping her comfortable. She's not eating much so my main focus is her comfort. I try to sleep, but I can hear the moans of pain and I immediately give her more medicine. Some days have come and gone before I realize I haven't even eaten." I don't know how my mind could have been caught up in the possible existence of a romance between Anne and Armin when Anne was dealing with so much. We sat quietly for just a moment until the silence became too uncomfortable. We lapsed back into a generic conversation, a brief one, and I took my leave. I left Anne with a heavy heart, I'm not sure why... maybe our visit just confirmed that I really had lost my friends to life. As I pedaled my bicycle back through our town, I slowed down to really take in what was happening around me. I took a long look at what I surely must have seen before. People trying to get their rationed foods, men gathered together looking at the newspaper with some shaking their heads and others shaking their fists. Had I just ignored it all in my youthful mind? I had always been safe and well-cared for as had my friends. How did we enjoy our days at school and graduation and our parties without seeing and knowing what was unfolding right beneath our noses? We all had Jewish friends or acquaintances. We knew that they had experienced a difficult time in 1938 during Kristallnacht when their synagogue on Michelsberg was destroyed. But, even this had not cracked our veneer. We were still in school. We were still enjoying our homes and our own churches. We were fine. We had not been born into the real world yet, we were still safe in our cocoons. Or, were we…or maybe me… just that obtuse? Was it a matter of whether or not we noticed the world around us or was it a matter of we did, and chose not to? I was embarrassed to even admit to myself that I had been the proverbial ostrich with its head in the sand. Now that I had decided to peek out from the sand, nothing was the same as when I went into hiding. Whatever it was, I realized I was just waking up and I felt the sleep falling away from my eyelids. As I watched some of the soldiers of the 53rd squadron of the Luftwaffe hanging about in town, I knew in my heart that a changed world was being ushered in by this war and whether I was ready or not, it was time to join real life.

CHAPTER THREE

MAY 2011

"Happy birthday to you, happy birthday to you, happy birthday Ms. Effie, happy birthday to you! And many more! Blow out your candle Ms. Effie and be sure to make a wish!" Pam sang out in her completely off-key, tone-deaf voice that was beautifully filled with love.

"Oh, my goodness, what a sinfully delicious looking cupcake, Pam! Where on earth did you ever find such a huge cupcake?" My mouth was literally watering as I sat looking at the biggest swirl of fluffy chocolate icing with a shower of colorful sprinkles on top that I had ever seen. Chocolate had always been such a weakness for me!

"We have the neatest little cupcake bakery on my way to work. Here's a napkin, dig in Ms. Effie, they are soooo good!"

"You are going to have to half this with me!" I mumbled around a very un-ladylike bite of cake. I closed my eyes as I held the rich moist cake in my mouth and let the super-sweet dark chocolate icing melt in my mouth. My taste buds might as well have been 18 instead of 89.

"It's all you Ms. Effie. I'm going to get rid of this fluff around my middle before bathing suit weather."

I wiped my mouth and tried to pry my mind off of one of my greatest joys- eating chocolate. "Oh please, you're as tiny as can be already. But, if you don't want any I'm going to have to save some for later. It is so good though, and is definitely home-made just like Mama used to make. Thank you, Pam, for making an old ladies' day." Yes, I was really letting sappiness drift into my special day.

"Ms. Effie, it's my pleasure. You know I enjoy being with you, how could I let your birthday go by without doing something. Are your children coming today?"

"No, they both called though." I quickly acknowledged the two obligatory calls that took place; nearly simultaneously, this morning. "And between my big lunch of all my favorite carbohydrates and now this cupcake, I think I could lie down and catch a few winks."

"Ok Ms. Effie, you go on ahead and take a nap. I'll check on you in a bit."

I made my way slowly to my room, cupcake in one hand and birthday hat in the other. I couldn't believe I was 89. Shouldn't there be some kind of trophy or something for surviving this long? As I put my cake on my nightstand and climbed onto my neatly made bed, I of course drifted back over my previous birthdays. What else was an 89-year-old supposed to think about? I thought about all that had happened since my 18th "biggie" birthday as Anne had called it. I thought about meeting Lucy.

October 1940

I had made up my mind that I was going to take some kind of action and get involved in the world around me. I was waiting in my Papa's study one late afternoon thinking how to approach him about volunteering in some realm. Since my visit with Anne I had been trying to find some way to get involved. Seeing her, Armin, Brigitte all moving on with their lives made me feel like I had a lot of catching up to do. I had discovered that there were lots of places either taking volunteers or actually hiring girls to work in offices or clinics or train as nurse aids. I had the usual skills of typing and filing and I also spoke three languages, German of course, English and French. Surely these attributes would secure a position for me somewhere.

"Oh, Effie, I didn't know you were in here. Quiet as my Little Mouse!" My father, tall, trim built with a thick shock of black hair that waved across his forehead and crystal clear blue eyes looked out behind his wire-rimmed glasses. He had all kinds of nick names for me, Little Mouse was just one of them. I would say that I had always turned to my father more than my mother. My mother was certainly a wonderful person, but my father was my Papa, my hero, my protector and my spoiler.

"I was just waiting to talk to you."

"Well, that certainly sounds ominous." Papa gave me a wink and took a seat behind his desk. I stood shuffling one food across the edge of the rug while I twirled my hair. Not exactly the stance I needed to take to propose such an adult question. "Papa, you know when I went to visit Anne the other day I started feeling like I'm being left behind. All of my friends have moved on and I am still here…doing the same things except going to school every day. Brigitte is actually involved in the war by training and working as a nurse, Armin and Sepp are part of the SS, Anne would be going down the same path if her mother weren't sick. I am over 18 (as though he would have forgotten) and I was thinking, I mean, I believe that…well…I think I should get a job or volunteer somewhere. I think I should be more involved with the war effort. I'm doing nothing! Just going from one day to the next floating along while everyone else is serving some purpose!"

"Well, now, I wouldn't say you were doing nothing. You help Mama here and you take meals to the ladies that are shut-ins. I think you are quite productive for a young lady. I'm sure you will meet some young man soon, unless Armin could turn your eyes in his direction, and you will be doing your part by raising your family."

"WHAT??" I screamed silently to myself. What could my father be thinking? Get married; have children when the world around us was at war? Did he think I was completely unaware of my surroundings? He viewed me as the child who only knew about their immediate world; nothing beyond my inner circle of friends. I had to regain my composure before I stomped my foot and stuck out my lip to get my way.

"Yes, well, Armin is quite taken with Anne and I'm happy for that. And so many of the guys that I may be interested in are gone right now…. so….in the meantime…I really feel that I should be doing something, maybe with the Red Cross."

"Effie, I really think you should stay close to home, especially for Mama. Why don't you come to the bank? I'm sure you would be very helpful there."

Of course. A nice place for a nice girl until I could be nicely placed in a nice marriage and home. He did realize we were in the middle of a war, didn't he? Granted, I had not been overly zealous in keeping up with all the ins and outs of the war, but I certainly wasn't completely unaware of the fact that Hitler had an unwavering agenda, I knew that Jewish people were being taken to housing facilities to work until the war ended. I also knew that not everyone thought that was what went on at those camps. I had overheard one of neighbors talking in a low voice to our other neighbor that they had heard the men and women were being separated and even the children. She said they were considered political criminals, but for what crimes? I know that we were supposed to think of ourselves as superior, but I just really couldn't think or feel that way. How silly to think one person was superior to another! But, who was I to question the direction Hitler wanted to take our country in? All I knew was that the war was ushering in changes that I didn't agree with and the more I heard and saw, the more I began to feel the injustices that were being heaped on the Jews around us. I didn't see myself as taking on some radical role, but I wanted to be doing something! Maybe if I were volunteering I would feel useful. Maybe there was a way to help some of the poor Jewish families that were being separated. I don't even know where that particular thought came from, but as I let it settle in my mind, it didn't seem like such a bad idea.

"Papa, I just can't sit around playing at life with all that is happening with this war on each side! I want to do *something*! I could be volunteering or working helping other people in some way. Maybe help some of our poor Jewish friends. Do you know what happens in those work-camps? Do you *really know*?" Yes, I screamed inwardly, I do know about some of it! And now that I have lost my temper and blurted this out, he would never let me out of the house to do anything! I could see the change come into his eyes. He knew he couldn't appease me with a pat on the head and a 'run along now'.

"Effie, I can appreciate that you have a helpful nature, but really, I think you are suffering more from boredom than anything. I know you miss your friends and the fun times you had, but it just can't be that way right now. That doesn't mean you have to do something extreme. Now, like I said, something at the bank, maybe at the newspaper would suite you just fine." Papa completed his statement the way he always did when he thought the conversation should be over. This, of course, pricked my temper. Here I finally figure out that I needed…wanted to do something worthwhile and Papa just wants to douse it out like a bothersome flame. Inwardly I was stamping my foot with fists at my sides, but I knew enough that displaying that stance he would prove himself right. "Papa! Please listen to me! I don't want to be tucked away or find a little job that my father actually secured for me! I want to do something that matters…the more I think of it the more I realize I'm not happy about what is going on and I want to take a stand…maybe if more people who have questions about what is happening to people would speak up, we could make a difference!"

"These are not things for you to be thinking about let alone speak about! Now stop this before you ever get started! You must never speak like this or question our leaders! We are safe now…please…no more of this kind of talk! This is NOT your business! This war is so much bigger than you know, please, just do what I say Effie! I don't want to hear any more about it! You either stay home and continue to help Mama, or you let me find something. That's it!"

I was stunned. I had never heard my father raise his voice to me like that. Nor had I ever seen him look at me like that. I saw my father, my childhood hero standing not quite as tall as he once had, his strong as steel hands hanging helpless at his sides. I saw his eyes, the ones that always looked at me with a mixture of love, humor, and curiosity. They now looked at me in …fear and anger. I could see his pulse throbbing in his neck. I could hear my own pulse pounding in my ears. We were suddenly at a crossroads. I had never dared to so much as disagree with my father.… nor he with me…I stood with my mouth slightly open, completely dry, my heart accelerating and millions of thoughts rushed through my mind. I blinked and slowly looked from my father around the study. I took in the large oak desk, the dark brown leather chairs, and the fire place that doubled as a backdrop for our Christmas pictures. I saw the smoke rising from the pipe in the ashtray that he had been smoking and I could smell the rich cherry tobacco that burned in it. My eyes slowly turned back to my father. He was unyielding. Whatever he knew, whatever he had seen, must have scared or angered him so much that he absolutely could not tolerate this line of conversation. I licked my lips and took a slow deep breath. It wasn't so much what he said that stunned me, but the tone of his voice and the expression on his face.

"Papa, I'm sorry. I didn't mean to upset you…it's just that I feel something really bad could be happening…"

"Effie, stop it, NOW!" he crossed the room and grabbed my hand and pulled me through the double doors leading to the outside patio. In a coarse whisper he said, "You know nothing! You don't know what is going on or why! You don't know who could be listening. Do you know what people are called who help the Jews…sympathizers…do you know how dangerous it is to be called that? You must never be thought of as a sympathizer! We will not discuss this again, do you understand? Yes, I believe bad things are happening with this war, as with all wars. We must do whatever we have to do in order to keep our family together and safe. Please do not add to my list of worries!" He had sweat beading up around his mouth and his grip on my hand was like a vice. My father never lost his composure and was always the peace-maker. He looked panicked. I immediately felt sorry that I had peaked my father's anger like this. I had never upset him like this and now that I had, it would extremely difficult if not impossible to involve myself with anything I thought of as useful.

"I'm so sorry Papa; of course, I wouldn't want to do that! I was just feeling useless. I won't bring it up again, I promise!" I declared the first lie in a long line of lies to my father.

CHAPTER FOUR

LUCY

I slipped out the patio door later that evening, well before curfew, under the pretense of going to stay with Anneliese for the night. So, as we finished dinner that night I was surprised when I asked if I could spend the night with Anne that Papa actually agreed. Maybe he thought I would forget about our conversation earlier if I occupied my time with my friend. He must have still thought we sat around and put pin curls in each other's hair and painted our nails when we got together. I was in fact going to eventually end my wanderings there, but I had to let my father's outburst sink in and try to make sense of it. I wanted to see what was going on in town, what the guys from the Luftwaffe did in the evenings. I can't say why, just curiosity. It was nearing dusk as I walked past the Marktkirche and took the path that curved behind its majestic neo-Gothic façade. The temperature had dropped and the air was crisp and so full of the scents of the surrounding café's and bakeries that it made my stomach growl even though I had already eaten. They were preparing breads, dumplings, pastries, and pies for evening meals as well as fresh loaves for the next morning. I loved my hometown, I loved the German food, and I loved being German. Did that mean I had to hate everyone else? I passed by one road that had one or two cafés'. We had always known these cafés had been there and were known for their boisterous night life, but had never felt the pull to go in. There was one café that must have been more beer hall than café and I could hear the laughter and singing well before I approached the entrance. What on earth I thought I was going to do, I have no idea. I was out of my league by even walking close to the beer hall. My head said, "Just keep walking…just go straight to Anne's house."

That message never reached my feet. There were a handful of tables outside in the front. There lingered uniformed men and ladies sitting with them, made-up with hair curled up high and bright red lips and nails. They were smoking, drinking, and laughing, but mostly flirting. What were my traitorous legs doing carrying me toward this scene? I could smell the cigarette and cigar smoke wafting through the air as well as the heavy sweet floral scent of perfume enticing the male species to lean closer to the hunters. My palms were sweaty and small beads were gathering on my top lip, even with the cool air. This was not the type of place my friends and I would be before the war. My eyes were starting to sting from the smoke in the air. Every warning bell and every voice in my head was screaming for me to turn around and go to Anne's. I was walking past the tables and straight into the front door and into a crowd of people that were somehow oblivious to me being a complete outsider. Now what? I tried to stick my nose slightly higher in the air as I looked around to give off an appearance of maturity. The place was packed with uniformed and non-uniformed guys and probably twice as many women. The smoke was thick and there was an unprofessional symphony of beer glasses clanking together and high-pitched laughter combined with the alto and base of men trying to be impressive. What was I doing here? Just when the fog started to lift and I was becoming cognizant of the fact that I needed to leave, my eyes lit on a lady's face. Her eyes were glistening and…. laughing. Her eyes were actually laughing at me. She had a "cat that ate the canary" smile and an air of knowing exactly what a fool I was making of myself. I must have suddenly looked even more pathetic as I tried to back up and turn around in the crowd that it caused her laughter to travel from her eyes and come bubbling out of her mouth. She all at once took pity on me and shouted over the crowd while she waived me over, "There you are! I have been waiting for you…come this way!"

Do I risk pointing at my chest and asking "me?" or do I look behind me to make sure she's talking to me? No, I just walk over to her bumping into several couples along the way. This bright-eyed, blond-haired flashy lady grasped my hand and leaned into my ear, "Act like you know what you are doing and this is exactly where you want to be."

I attempted a smile and stammered, "Thanks for waiting for me…. I was…uh…hoping not to make you wait too long."

"Something to drink? Beer, vodka?"

"No…I.um….. yes, vodka would be…ok." WHAT? I have never had anything like that to drink!

"Let's go over to this table." The platinum diva led us to a bistro table in the furthest corner from the bar. She was bathed in lingering smiles and glances from several guys as we weaved our way through the crowd.

"I'm Lucy. Now, who are you and what on earth are you doing in here? You are still fairly young, and I'm guessing this is a first. You are looking for a romance with a soldier maybe?" She gave me a quick wink.

"My name is Effie, and no, I'm not looking for a romance. I really don't know why I came in here. I'm on my way to my friends on Grabenstrabe. I'm just walking."

"You looked lost. Are you sure you aren't looking for someone?"

This was so out of character for me. What was I looking for? I had taken several sips of my drink. We normally drank wine and this was affecting me somewhat differently. When I say we normally drank wine what I really mean is I tried it at a couple of parties. I was most definitely a novice. "I'm from here…I've just never been in *here*. I was walking to my friends' and thought I would see what it was like in here." What on earth would my sweet Papa think if he knew where I was? I had never rebelled against my mother or father. I don't know what was getting into me. I sat with my hands cupped around the drink and looked around at all the laughing and flirting couples. One would think there was nothing serious happening outside these doors, as if the crisp uniforms were a fashion statement. Lucy pulled out a compact and mirror from her bag and dabbed at her mouth, careful to not wipe off her cherry red lipstick. "So, what do you do? Are you a student?"

I responded with a generic response. "I'm looking for a job…maybe volunteer somewhere. I finished school last year."

"I see." Lucy replied as she gazed straight into my eyes. That's it? 'I see'? What happened to Ms. All-Knowing? Finally, the wise one spoke, "I'm guessing you have recently finished school, that you are proficient in multiple languages, and can possibly type and file…am I close?"

"Yes, of course!" I said somewhat defiantly

"Maybe you could work with me. We need plenty of office girls."

"Where? What do you do?"

23

"I work with the 53rd. I'm an office girl too. It's a job and I'm doing my part. Plus, you meet some interesting people. Or, there is always the Red Cross, as I'm sure you know."

"No, I can't do that. I'm not sure. I don't know how my father would feel about me working there."

"My cousin owns a clothing store nearby. They repair uniforms and such. Maybe that would be more for you. Think about it. I can help you. I will be here tomorrow night. You decide, and I will help." I nodded my understanding, not necessarily an agreement to meet. First of all, I would have to ask to get a job somewhere besides the bank and I had already seen where that conversation could lead. Second, I wasn't sure about Lucy. We just met and she's offering to help me with a job. Maybe I should just forget all of this and do exactly what my father suggested and wait the war out and go on with my life. Sitting in this café with an obviously older and more sophisticated person shrunk my bravado significantly. Just at that moment I saw Lucy's smile take on the look of the Cheshire cat who not only ate the canary, but was looking for another. Her eyes cast a glance toward me, "Well, for right now, it looks like romance is looking for you whether you are or not." Lucy slightly inclined her head to my left. Not being practiced at non-chalant behavior I quickly looked to my left and first saw the most beautiful face on a man that I had ever seen; and second I saw the uniform that was attached to him. I flushed from the alcohol, the intense stare or both. He didn't move toward us, but the overt stare diminished any space or person that was between us. True to my juvenile form it took me literally minutes to drag my eyes from his and back to Lucy, who was once again wearing the wiser than Solomon expression.

"That is Emmerick Amsel. He is an officer. I see him at the 53rd from time to time. Maybe better scenery there than my cousins' shop." Lucy grinned and raised her glass toward Emmerick.

I was dumb-struck. Sometimes even I felt my own young age stand out like a flashing sign. I would not have been surprised if my mouth were hanging open. I had been on dates, of course, but only with boys my age. This Emmerick looked several years older than me...and.. those eyes... whew! I turned back to the table and Lucy. "Does he know you? Do you talk to him?"

"Yes, I know him and we talk. It's not like that though, he's definitely not my type."

"Are you kidding? He's *every girl's type!*" I took a chance to glance back over my shoulder in time to see him move on to another group. "Well, I probably need to get going. Thanks again, and I will think about what you said." I opened my purse to pay for the unfinished drink as I thanked Lucy for saving me from my embarrassing entrance. She repeated her offer to help me find a job and I stood, this time never looking to my left. Somehow, I made it out of the café and back into the cool air without tripping or spilling anyone's drink or drawing unwanted attention. I didn't have much time to get up Marktsrabe and over to Grabenstrabe and to Anne's home. As my heels clicked over the damp cobble-stone streets, Lucy's words played continuously in my mind. Was this the path I needed to take? Would this lead me to a way of really helping people or would I just be helping the SS do what I was hoping to avoid? And how on earth would I ever going to convince my father to let me do this? Maybe if he thought I would be working with the milliner...lies were starting to formulate much quicker and easier in my mind.

CHAPTER FIVE

Anne was able to relax more that evening and it was almost like a sleepover we would have had in school. I told her all about the conversation with my father, walking into the beer hall, (which elicited the highest eyebrow on her face I had ever seen), meeting Lucy and about the offer to help me get a job. Anne and I concocted several scenarios that I thought my father would accept. In the end, I opted for a father friendly version of the truth. With a little fabricating session with Anne I came up with a job opportunity mentioned to her by Armin (an apple in Papa's eye) that I might be interested in. It was to be "just an office girl" job, but duties behind the scenes that needed to be done. We perfected my proposal and shockingly I was able to deliver my speech to my father, who in turn actually said I could give it a try, but he also strongly admonished me to not show any behaviors that could lead someone working with me to think I was on the fence about Jews. Now that I had permission to try for the job, I was a little afraid of what I was actually getting myself into.

Lucy had been true to her word and she was able to get me an interview and with a few pointers on interviewing skills, I was given a job and a desk just a few away from hers. It was a small room in one wing of a building attached to the 53rd. On every desk, there was a typewriter and a set of headphones, paper tablets and pens. On the corner sat a metal wire basket. We were responsible for typing propaganda sheets as we listened to speeches made by the fuehrer and other high-ranking officials. My work day began at eight and ended at four-thirty. I wore my pencil thin skirts, tailored jackets with the military style shoulder pads and cinched waists. These outfits were topped off with my leather pumps, gloves, hat and handbag. Along with Lucy's interview tutoring, she also gave me instructions for wearing make-up. I rarely wore any before then, but Lucy thought it would help me look a little more sophisticated and polished. So, every morning I began a new, nearly religious routine of applying my bisque face powder, a thin black line on my eyelids, black mascara and to top it off deep, cherry red lipstick. Lucy, in all her fashion wisdom informed me that this lipstick was all the rage. She educated me in the knowledge granted to one from years of studying the products, that an American cosmetics designer had designed this lipstick, Montezuma Red, in honor of the red trim on female Marines' uniforms. So, now I was set! I had a job, I was little Miss Sophisticate, and I was gaining that worldly knowledge needed by young women.

By the end of my third week I was feeling fairly proficient at transcribing speeches. I was also feeling sufficiently disgusted at some of what I was typing; however, some of the information was what had been repeated to us ever since we were youth. To me, as well as thousands of other Germans, much of the propaganda made sense. Some speeches simply promoted loyalty to country and man. Adolph Hitler and other officials were masters of inciting patriotism from the youngest to the oldest German. I had been working on transcribing a propaganda speech that was to accompany some posters and the part of the speech by the fuehrer that I typed had even ignited a spark of patriotic loyalty in me. "You are born into your people, my child, of a German mother – your father is a German. And you belong to the German people just as every part of your body belongs to you. You are a link in a great chain, a part of the whole. Alone, you are nothing, but when you live for your people you are everything. Your people's destiny is your destiny. Its struggles and sorrows, its joys and miseries, are yours. All Germans are your brothers. You may not think, want or do anything that harms your people! The history of your people is great and glorious and you can be proud of it."-Adolph Hitler. These powerfully zealous words spoken by the fuehrer would ignite fervor in anyone. We were only privileged, of course, to news from the Nazi Party's view. The year of 1940, particularly the summer months were full of military action. According to our information, the SS and Luftwaffe were unstoppable. German troops marched into Paris and Italy and declared war on France and Britain. What we heard loud and clear was the Luftwaffe was bombing the heck out of Great Britain, but the day we lost 76 aircraft obviously was not one of our "go ahead" broadcasts. It was surprising to me that conversations about the war, strategies, camps, and experimentation were so openly held. It was the assumption of course that everyone felt the same way, or at least knew better than to openly disagree.

The war was escalating at an alarming rate and so was my education. I had been hearing more "snippets" of information about medical experiments that were to take place at Ravensbruck as well as other work camps. I just couldn't believe all that I had heard; it was ridiculous to think they could be completely true! Yet, the sickening rumors of bone, muscle, and nerve transplants were being done without anesthesia. I was only ten when the law was passed, aesthetically labeled The Law for the Prevention of Genetically Defective Progeny; which prompted the physicians at Ravensbruck and Auschwitz to carry out sterilization projects. But I was Aryan, and young, so this never touched my life before. As children, we never even heard of such laws.

So, I found myself daily being torn. But in my heart, love of humanity was winning out over loyalty to this changing Germany. But as my father had warned me, I never mentioned or so much as let my face express surprise. I didn't even tell my mother or father details of some of what I was seeing and hearing.

I also found myself gravitating toward Lucy more every day. Not only had she helped me with this position, but she was funny and seemed to understand me and almost eerily read my mind. We took our noon breaks together nearly every day each bringing boiled eggs and baked bread, sometimes with jam and depending on rations, tea. Lucy would explain aspects of our jobs and asked tons of questions. This made me feel.... interesting and important. She asked about my family, what my father did for a living, and about my friends. Lucy was only a few years older than me, but I was totally in awe of her knowledge and life experience. She seemed to know everyone at our jobs and was liked by everyone, especially the officers. She confided in me details of how she grew up, where she attended school, guys she had dated. If there wasn't a war raging, one would think we were just two co-workers becoming close friends. Lucy introduced me to some of her close friends and after a couple of months of getting to know each other and some of her friends, she had invited me to a "get-together" at her apartment one Friday evening. She said there would be some people from work, but she didn't say exactly who. So, I vacillated all week between wanting to go and not wanting to go. I really liked Lucy and had started getting to know a few of the other girls, but she also knew several guys that could be there…one guy in particular. In the end, I was swayed to go and when Friday arrived I rushed home to get freshened up for the dinner. The summer was unusually hot, and I was hoping that my face wasn't melting off me and onto the pavement as I walked to the train station to get a ride to Lucy's apartment. I arrived with my face surprisingly still intact and offered to help Lucy in the kitchen. She claimed to have everything under control, and since I didn't cook I gladly left her to it. She leaned over to me and whispered while glancing out of the kitchen door, "your café crush is here. Come on, I will officially introduce you." I think it could have been an actual heart attack, even though I was young, healthy, and more on the under-weight side of the scales, I can safely say that when she nodded toward the beautiful-faced man from the café of our original meeting it was an actual heart attack that I felt. Maybe at least I could blame my flushed skin on the heat. The heat of having walked from the train station that is.

"Hey Emmerick, slide over, I want to introduce you to my friend. Emmerick Amsel, this is Effie Reinhardt. Effie, this is Emmerick. He works with the Luftwaffe, actually at the 53rd a great deal of the time. Effie, have a seat while I finish up." Lucy glided away from us and back to the safety of the kitchen, conveniently out of the reach of my two hands.

"So, Effie, I've seen you before. You probably don't remember me, but I saw you with Lucy at the café. It's been quite a while, but I remember you." The Greek god spoke. And I sat. Respond! Make your tongue form words in your mouth, I screamed at myself.

"Oh, well, I don't mean to be rude, but we see so many people when we are out." What the heck was I saying?! I didn't go out! He's going to see right through me!

"I apologize then for assuming I made an everlasting impression on you." He gave me a slightly lop-sided grin as if to say 'Ya, I made an impression and I know it.' Was it as hot in here as it was outside? Good grief Lucy, turn off the oven!

"So, you work with Lucy? And how do you like it?" He just kept on going with his perfect voice coming out of his perfect face.

"I don't…I…I mean I do! Like it that is. Lucy is great! I'm learning a lot. I feel like I'm making a contribution." I'm an idiot, that's what I am Emmerick! Can't you see that I barely know how to speak!

To my surprise, Emmerick found me humorous. "Effie, relax. I'm not interrogating you. You seem like a very nice person. This is just a conversation between two people that work at the same place and know some of the same people. If I'm making you uncomfortable, I'm sorry. Now, just talk to me like I'm Lucy." Uh huh, ok "Lucy", I thought to myself…. see this gorgeous specimen I'm sitting next to? I want to marry him and live happily ever after. Isn't he the most beautiful creature? Oh, what did you say "Lucy", he loves me already? Of course, he does!

This line of thinking at least made me laugh at myself enough to allow me to talk with him with at least the intelligence of an eighth-grade girl. The night wore on and Lucy had the nerve to seat me next to him during dinner so by the end of the evening, and I was actually pretty fluent in my speech with Emmerick. I was completely star-struck! I relived the evening for the entire weekend. Not only had he made an impression on me at the café, but he had firmly planted his picture in my mind and nothing seemed to be important enough to replace it for days. Every time I mingled away to speak to Lucy or someone else I couldn't stop myself from trying to see where he was and if he happened to be looking for me too. Geez, just like being in school again!

The following Monday at our noon break Lucy was biting at the bit to talk to me. "So, looks like you and Emmerick hit it off pretty well. When you weren't sitting together, he was watching your every move. Are you going to see him again?" Lucy didn't waste any time asking questions.

"Yes…. I mean…no…yes, we seemed to hit it off, and he is just about the most perfect guy I have ever talked to, but I just don't know. He did ask if he could see me again. I didn't answer. It was pretty hard to speak clearly for the better part of the night. He's so much more… confident than the boys I knew in school. And he's so smart! But he isn't condescending when he's talking. But mostly, he's gorgeous!" I giggled like I was twelve!

Lucy laughed right along with me, "Well, he is pretty nice to look at, and he has always acted very much like a gentleman, why on earth wouldn't you go out with him? You aren't attached and he's clearly interested in you. What's holding you back? Does your papa not allow you to date seriously yet?" There…she had hopefully pricked Effie's pride enough to illicit a rebellious response. Lucy's tone was a little surprising almost as if she were talking down to me. Why was she being so pushy? What was it to her if we went out or not?

Lucy was sitting on the edge of her seat ready to pounce on the opportunity she had been waiting for. Effie was exactly the type of girl they were looking for. Now Lucy just needed to dangle Emmerick in front of her like the forbidden fruit. She could see that Effie was on the cusp of that time of life when one is trying to break away from their parents and become the adult that their age said they were. She could see that the night Effie wandered into the beer hall looking like a lost lamb. The fact that she obviously found Emmerick attractive from the first night would make it that much easier to pull her in.

"Well, honestly I haven't liked anyone enough to think of seriously dating. It really doesn't have anything to do with my parents' permission! And besides, one dinner doesn't mean we are dating at all seriously or otherwise. Sure, we did talk a lot the other night, but now that I think about it, we really only talked about me. I didn't even realize we weren't talking about him since I was mostly concentrating on his half smile and how he rolled up his sleeves." Just thinking about how attractive he was caused a flush to creep up my neck.

"So, what do you want to know? I've known him a long time I can tell you about him. He's really a nice guy Effie. Would you like to know about his parents, his family…his girlfriends?" Lucy said with a sly smile and a side long glance at Effie. "He's 23, he was born in Munich, his father passed away at the end of the Great War, Emmerick was only two. He is an only child, like you, and he is a hard worker. As far as girlfriends…he's never had to look very far, but let me assure you he's a gentleman."

Lucy's synopsis of Emmerick made me feel silly and childish for seeming so cautious. But that still didn't answer one of the questions I really had nipping at the edges of my mind. Was he truly one of 'them'? Did he ever work at the camps? It was hard to imagine him being cruel to anyone, but I had to remember what uniform he wore. How could I ask Lucy without drawing unwanted attention to my true feelings about the Jews? I supposed the best thing would have been to drop the conversation completely. I felt like I knew Lucy, but what if I was wrong? What if I said something that caused her to point me out to our supervisor or worse?

But since I had ignored the voice of reason in my head for the past several months, why should now be any different?

"Lucy, what does Emmerick do? Does he only work here? Do they ever send him to other places? I mean, how much does he have to do with the work camps?"

Ok Lucy, be careful with this one, she had to know for sure that she could be trusted. "What a question Effie. I suppose all the SS soldiers might have to eventually. Why? What difference does that make? What does it have to do with you going out with him?"

Maybe I had stepped over the line, but I couldn't stop myself now. If he did some of the things I had heard about at the camps there would be no way I could feel right about continuing to see him.

"He just seems like such a nice guy and I would like to get to know him better but it seems like the guys who do that, who work at the camps…well they might not be so…nice. They might be more…aggressive."

"Effie, I really don't think you would have anything to worry about with Emmerick. And the people at work camps are political prisoners, so why should that concern you?" Now all Lucy had to do was wait for the right response.

I sat quietly for a moment, trying to think of the least incriminating way to say that I had sympathy for the Jews. "Lucy, I am a German and so very proud to be so, but sometimes…I feel… I mean I would never question the fuehrer, but sometimes I feel a little sorry for the people that end up there." I nearly said this as an apology. I had no way of knowing that admission was the key to unlocking my future, the rest of my life really.

Lucy stared at me for what seemed like an eternity. She seemed to be reading my mind and making a decision all at the same time. Her next words were a carefully planned trap. They were a baited hook that I gladly swallowed and allowed myself to be pulled into the net. "You may not believe me Effie, but I actually feel the same way you do. I have wanted to share my feelings, but was afraid you would think me to be unpatriotic or worse. I love our country too, but I've also heard of the harsh treatment to people and I too have a hard time reconciling this treatment with the Germany I know. But you know you must be very careful who you say these things to. And I really hope that I haven't said too much to you. I trust you Effie to never say anything that I have said to anyone."

I felt immediately relieved…and even happy. I found someone that felt the same way and who I could trust. "Lucy, I was so scared to say anything! What a relief to know I can trust someone. This is what I meant when I said I wanted to help! I want to help those people, but I don't know how! I've tried to think of different ideas but everything I come up with is either ridiculous or just simply not possible. Maybe there isn't a way to help, but if I could do something meaningful and helpful I would feel like I was making a difference to someone."

"Well, calm down a little Effie. Like I said we have to be very careful! You have to watch what you say and where you say it. Now, I know how you feel…but we have to think this out carefully. And one more thing… we are not the only ones who feel this way. I won't tell you names just yet. But I will say this, if you like Emmerick, I think he is a fine individual. Lucy gave me a quick hug and a wink and said she needed to get back to work, but we could get together after work. As she walked away she turned back to me and put her finger up to her lips to remind me to be very quiet about what we had talked about. Lucy walked back to her desk with a very satisfied if not smug look on her face. It had almost been too easy. Effie was so young and innocent, Lucy thought she should even feel a little guilty. The trick now would be to contain her, to keep her from blurting out any of this to anyone else. Lucy felt that she had made sure Effie was being pulled in and that she was her only confidante. Now Lucy needed to educate Effie to the very real dangers of being a Jew sympathizer.

My mind raced the rest of the day. For moments, I questioned my decision to tell Lucy, but in the end, I still felt relieved. I could hardly wait to resume our conversation. And, did she really mean what I thought she meant about Emmerick? I sure hoped so, for one thing I would like to know we might have help on the inside and for another thing…well, he was very handsome.

The afternoon was passing too slowly and by quitting time I was about to spring out of my skin. My anticipated time with Lucy would have to wait though. Just as we were about to leave, Lucy said she was sorry but something had come up. Before she left she asked if I was really ready to help in the way I had said. She said she had some things in mind, but until she had them worked out she didn't want to get me involved. Lucy reassured me that we would start meeting away from work and asked me to pledge my secrecy one more time. "Effie, I can't express enough how dangerous this is… you have to keep this to yourself! Nobody can be told… not even your parents. I will deny our conversation Effie, if you say anything to anyone I will deny every bit of it."

In spite of the harsh admonition from Lucy, as I left work I had a brand-new feeling. I felt purposeful and alive. My heels clicked faster and faster as I walked through town toward home. The sounds hitting the pavement matched the pace of my heart.

I walked into the warmth of my home and followed the smell of dinner into the kitchen. Papa and Mother was there…Papa reading the newspaper while Mother stirred the source of the delicious smell.

"So young working lady, how was your day?" Papa asked as he looked over the top of his paper. "Pretty much the same Papa. Just typing paper-work." It now took no effort for a lie to slide smoothly between my lips.

CHAPTER SIX

Over the next several weeks, Lucy and I spent many evenings at her place talking about different ways that she had heard of people helping out some of the German Jews. She asked a lot of questions as well. She asked about my friends and started making suggestions that I try to glean information from them. I wasn't sure how that was supposed to help. But Lucy was mature and seemed to have been thinking about this for quite some time so I felt I needed to prove that I was ready for my new calling. I was trying to figure out what I was supposed to learn from my friends when we got the word from Anneliese, her mother had passed away. I had been so wrapped up in my job and new friendships that I had only been to see Anne a couple of times. Poor Anneliese! I immediately rode my bicycle to her home. I ran up the steps and barely knocked as I opened the door and went in. I could hear Anne talking low in the front room. I knocked on the door frame to the living room and looked in to see Anne sitting in the chair next to the fireplace and standing stoically next to her in a sharply creased uniform and black Hessian boots was Armin.

"Oh, Effie, please come in!" I reached out for my friend and grasped both her hands as I kneeled down in front of her. "How on earth are you holding up?" I asked without making eye contact with Armin. Anne released my hands and automatically reached up and touched Armin's hand that was resting protectively on her shoulder. "Of course, we have been expecting this, but that really doesn't make it any easier."

"No, I'm sure it doesn't. What can I do for you? Mother said she would be bringing meals for you. I can come stay with you." All of a sudden, I felt the weight of the fact that I really had not been there for my one-time best friend.

"Effie, there's really nothing to be done. The arrangements were made weeks ago. Armin has been very helpful with all the details. It's just good to have you here."

After nearly 30 minutes of awkward conversation, I stood and hugged her and gave a quick smile to Armin. I told her I would be back the next day and of course my family and I would be at the services. Things certainly had changed. I never seriously dated Armin, but before the war we still spoke friendly to each other. His stance and his silence were almost challenging. It was as if he were daring me to come between himself and Anne. It was such a strange feeling.

CHAPTER SEVEN

Anneliese's mother had lived her last months and possibly years feeling nearly deserted, but one would have never known that by the multitude that turned out at the funeral service. There were her relatives and even Anne's father and his relatives and of course all of Anne's friends. I don't know if I felt like an outsider because of my dual allegiance or if my friends were really pulling away from me. They seemed to keep me on the perimeter of their conversation, but not directly in them. Armin barely left Anne's side and Brigitte, Axel and Sepp huddled together. I was propped on the doorway between the living room and kitchen holding a cup of tea, just close enough to slightly hear their conversation and to any onlooker appear to be part of the group. Even my hot tea could not have stopped my blood from chilling as I listened to their calloused conversation.

"I can't believe how privileged I am to be witnessing the unbelievable discoveries that the doctors are making. We were always taught that we were the pure race with pure blood, and they will finally prove that to the world of science." Brigitte's eyes were glowing and she spoke with the type of excitement a bride uses to describe her groom. The guys were tapping their cups together in a congratulatory movement. I could not believe my eyes or ears. First of all, we were there to support Anne while she grieved and second, I could not believe how many levels they were wrong on. We were supposed to be here to comfort a friend and they couldn't let their politics go long enough to accomplish even that. These could not be the same people I grew up with. How could their hearts have so easily turned to blackness and evil? I may not have been as faithful to the teachings of my church as I could have been, but even I knew that this was not what God taught.

I suddenly felt sweaty and chilled all at the same time. Just at that time,

Lucy's face popped into my mind and I knew immediately that I needed to stop questioning and keep listening for any details that might help us save someone. I turned my attention back to the group and plastered a generic expression on my face. Axel leaned in closer to the group and said, "I can't say much, but just know that in a few months, possibly weeks, we will be sending you some more lab rats. We are finally going to cleanse our own hometown of the vermin."

Brigitte asked with glassy eyes, "Are they definitely coming to Ravensbruck?"

"Too many ears here, but I would say that you will have plenty of specimens to experiment on until your heart's content."

Before anymore was said, Anne and Armin came into the room to thank everyone for coming. I sat my tea cup down; miraculously I had not dropped it listening to their disgusting conversation. I meekly walked around the group and lightly touched Anne's arm. She turned and smiled through her tears and leaned over and kissed me on the cheek.

"Anne, if there's anything I can do, please let me know. I love you and I'm sorry for your loss." And I meant it, I did love Anne, but what on earth had I ever felt for the rest of the group? "I've got to head home but Mother and I will be back to help clean tomorrow."

Suddenly Sepp stepped over and placed his hand at my elbow. "I believe your parents already left. I will walk you home."

"Oh. Well, Sepp thank you, but that's really not necessary."

"I insist. You never know what kind of riffraff is out and about until we can clear out our area."

Not wanting to appear ungrateful I just nodded and allowed him to walk me to the door and beyond the light of the house. It was such an eerie feeling. Had he been watching me and my parents? How else could he have known they left?

As we walked, Sepp was the first to break the silence. "It's a sad time for Anneliese."

"Yes, I feel awful for her. Even though it was expected, it's a terrible loss."

"One never knows…especially in this day and age…how long we will have our loved ones. We should grasp every moment."

Sepp was speaking so cryptically. I was wondering what he could be alluding to as he continued to speak. "I know that you and I have never been the closest of friends in our group, but I had always hoped that we could be…. close."

I was totally caught off guard. I had no idea what to say. And his tone was so edgy, what he was saying almost sounded sinister. "Well, Sepp, I apologize if I have ever done anything to make you feel that we weren't friends."

Sepp gave a small condescending chuckle, "No, Effie, I'm sure you have not. The fault is mine, but maybe you will let me correct that."

"Sepp there is no fault. Let's just agree that maybe circumstances never allowed it. We are nearly to my house, I feel bad that you have to walk all the way back, I can make it from here. Why don't you head back to Anne's?"

"Effie, I'm going to be leaving in a few weeks and I don't want to let this opportunity to slip by."

"I don't understand…" Just as I was trying to speak, Sepp's face changed and his eyes darted up and down the street. His breathing was speeding up and he tightened his grip on my upper arm and started pulling me toward a vacant lot between two buildings. I was startled and started to protest when he pushed my back up next to the cold damp wall of one of the buildings and mashed his course dry lips next to mine, crushing and bruising them. I pushed at his chest but he was as solid as the wall behind me. He kept me pinned to the wall while continuing to push his lips on mine. He tried to intrude further into my mouth and as I tried to turn my head he grabbed my face and growled "Open your mouth!! You gave it freely to Armin, now it's my turn!!"

I pushed and pushed and turned my head just enough to let out a scream. He clamped his sweaty hand over my mouth. "Stop it! Shut up!!" I could hear voices at the end of the alley. "Now look what you've done!" He pulled me from the wall and gave me a shove so hard that I nearly fell. "Go on! Go home, but you won't always be so selfish with me!"

He growled some other threats but my blood was pounding in my ears as I tried to run in my heels toward home. Tears were blinding my vision and sobs were stuck in my throat choking me. I never looked back and after running for what seemed an eternity, I saw the front door of my home. I stopped and leaned on the door and I gave in to the torrent of tears. What

41

had just happened? I couldn't wrap my mind around the scene. How had a funeral service turned into an attack? It was all just too much, first Anne's mother, then the horrifying conversation and now this. I was shivering almost violently as I opened the door as quietly as possible. I can't explain why, but I didn't want my parents to know what had just happened. Had I encouraged him in some way? I couldn't even remember a time that we even had a singular conversation. As luck would have it, I was able to make it to my room, change, and then to the bathroom to scrub my face and brush my teeth several times before my mother knocked on the door. "Effie, we didn't hear you come in, are you alright?"

"Yes, I'm ok. It's just been an exhausting day." I was barely able to make my voice steady enough to reply.

"I know you feel bad for Anne as we all do. We will go back in the morning. Effie?"

"Yes Mother?"

"I love you."

"I love you too!" The sobs were unstoppable, and I'm sure my mother thought they were for Anne, as they should have been.

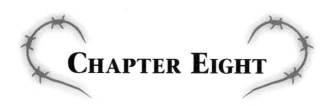

CHAPTER EIGHT

OCTOBER, 2011

"Ms., Effie?"

A young voice penetrated my semi-sleep world that I stayed in so many hours of the day. "Hhmm?" I replied with the absolute least amount of effort possible.

"Ms. Effie, you have company in the sun-room. I came to help you get ready." One would think this would make me happy, but apparently, I'm getting as old and grouchy as a winterized brown bear being poked at.

"Oh, Pam, just tell the ladies' group I don't feel like a visit today."

"It's not the ladies' group, it's your daughter."

I stopped my protesting, what on earth? Jonathon and Ruthie visited at Easter, Christmas, and Mothers Day, but this was just a Tuesday.... no wait...a Wednesday, no definitely a Tuesday. "Really? Is something wrong?"

"I don't think so; I just know she's waiting for you."

"Well, we better get down there!" Pam helped me with my sweater, combed my hair and handed me my lipstick. We walked as briskly as my nearly fossilized legs would carry me to the sun-room. She was standing staring out the window with her back to the door, looking neat as a pin. She always tried to look her best. Maybe she did inherit characteristics from me, like it or not.

"Ruthie?" She turned and looked at me with eyes so brown they were nearly black.

"Mother." Just a statement. Now that we recognized each other, maybe I could find out why she was here.

"What a lovely surprise! It's good to see you." I meant it. I loved my strong-willed daughter.

"Well, I have been meaning to come by; you know how it is with the kids and grandchildren."

"Of course, Ruthie, I know how demanding your life is. Is something wrong? Are you and the children alright?" Warning bells were beginning to sway back and forth in my mind.

"We are all fine. I just wanted to talk to you."

"Ok, let's sit down though these old limbs are beginning to protest."

"Mine are becoming disagreeable as well." We had a small moment of light laughter as we sat in the chairs in front of the window.

"So, what's on your mind Ruth?"

"Well…you know that I was going to start going through the house to organize things before we sell."

I had decided to sell my home last year with much approval from my children, but also with the understanding that I would be there to go through my own things. Before my husband died, he made me promise to only keep our house as long as I could take care of it. He always wanted me to be taken care of. "I knew WE would be organizing the house to get ready to sell."

"Mother, I had planned on taking you out there, and still will, but I just wanted to get an overall picture of what needs to be done."

"I appreciate your effort, Ruth, but I would rather be there when this takes place."

"It's a lot for you to do Mother. Anyway, I already decided I didn't need to be there without you. I came to see when you would feel like going."

"Oh. Well, my schedule is pretty flexible." I tried a pitiful attempt to lighten the mood. This conversation could have easily taken place by phone, there had to be something else that prompted Ruth to come in person. "You said you already realized I need to be there when you go back, and I agree whole-heartedly, but why do you suddenly feel that way?"

"I realized as I was walking through the house there are a lot of things I wouldn't know about. I wouldn't know the importance they hold for you."

"Yes…. that's why I wanted to be there. Ruthie, what is it? You are my most straight forward child and I find it rather disconcerting that you are beating behind the proverbial bush. Is it bothering you more than you thought to be selling the house? You know that you and Jonathon can have any furniture or anything else for that matter. What's really going on here?"

Maybe my strong as steel daughter did have a more sentimental side.

"I found some things that I've never seen before at the house."

"What? Where did you find them?"

"Umm, well, there was a beautiful lead crystal box, maybe a jewelry box because it looked like a piece of jewelry and maybe some important papers, I assumed it was something of Father's. It just reminded me that there's more than furniture there to go through. That's all."

"You didn't find those giving the house a "once over"! Did you read any of it?! These things are personal! You were snooping!!" I was livid! As if I had not lost enough already, but to have my own daughter invading my personal world!

"Mother, calm down! I didn't read anything. It's because I'm respecting your privacy that I stopped. It just made me think of my parents having more personal things than the average vase or picture frames."

"You weren't respecting it when you went into my room, subsequently unlocked my desk and pulled these things out!" We sat breathing and staring. Finally, Ruth broke the silence, "Look, I'm sorry. I won't go back up without you. When do you want to go?"

I didn't want to go at all now. I sat back in my chair and crossed my arms, "Did you put my things back? May I have the keys please? I will call you when I'm ready to go."

Sighing deeply, Ruth replied "Yes and yes. Here, I brought them with me. I really am sorry, obviously, curiosity almost got the better of me. There are things I don't know about my own mother and that's fine, my kids don't know everything about me either. Just call me when you are ready and I will take you."

Ruthie handed me the keys, and I looked into her eyes. My daughter.

I stayed in the sunroom long after Ruth left. I realized I had reacted all wrong in that situation. I behaved more like a child stamping their foot than an old lady. I just missed a perfect opportunity to share some of our history. The best time would be when the kids were together, but I needed to start somewhere and today I blew another chance. Just as I was berating myself for another missed chance to really talk to my daughter, Pam came in to let me know she was leaving for the day and wondered if I wanted her to help me back to my room.

"You ok Miss Effie? You've been out here a while. Did you have a good visit with Miss Ruth?"

I faintly smiled at the irony of her question. "Oh, yes, it's always nice to see her. But you go ahead and go home, I think I will stay out here a bit."

"Feel like more stories? You and my other residents have had the most interesting lives. I love hearing about the old days, it makes me wish I had lived back then." Pam asks innocently.

I patted her hand like an old grand-motherly type would do, "I'm a little spent today Pam. Maybe another day. Besides, you have plenty of fun things to do outside of this place! You go ahead. I will see you tomorrow."

Pam grinned and gave my old wrinkled hand a squeeze as she left for the day. I couldn't help but think how wrong she was. She only knows the nostalgic stories I have told her, not even skimming the surface of the brutal truth of those days. It makes me almost regret sharing any stories with her because I have misled her into thinking everything was so romantic back then. I can't say why I was spending the time to revisit those days with Pam instead of my own kids.... a situation I would need to correct.

CHAPTER NINE

EMMERICK

It surprised me that I could look at a male with anything but disgust after Sepp's unwanted advances, but as it turned out, the more time I spent with Emmerick, I realized that I not only didn't look at him with disgust, but with fascination. We had been meeting regularly ever since the funeral. I passed on all that I had heard at Anne's house. Emmerick said that thanks to my information, "they" were able to help several Jewish families avoid that particular roundup. I didn't know who "they" were. And there were other questions that were always trying to implant themselves firmly into my mind trying to not be ignored, but ignore them I did. I just knew that Lucy, and even more so Emmerick seemed to value my input, my opinions and ideas. Lucy had been leaving the meetings earlier and earlier giving Emmerick and myself more time to get acquainted. We ended up having long conversations that almost always revolved around me. This was such a magical drug, that all my senses were heightened when I was with him. My eyes saw every time his eyes would get that mischievous look followed by the little wrinkles that appeared at their corners that subsequently tugged the edges of his mouth upwards into that clichéd heart melting smile. His smile was beautiful. He had full lips and straight white teeth. Most of the time we met in the evenings so he always had that dark shadow of stubble showing up. He had strong looking hands that looked work roughened and calloused. And when he would roll up his sleeves showing his forearms, well it was nearly my undoing. I don't know what kind of cologne he wore, but my nose could have identified that smell anywhere. Up until then I didn't know that the smell of a man could cause an actual physical reaction, but it did. The first smell caused a stream of lava to slowly flow from my core downward. And his voice… I know I probably missed a lot of what he said from listening to *how* he said it. I was so infatuated with him that everything he said was right, and I was quickly becoming as much of a blind mouse as the ones that followed the Pied Piper. Especially after the First Kiss. It had been after dinner one night, Lucy had already gone home. I have forgotten many things over the years, but I will never forget the feel of his hands on each side of my face, warm and coarse; the way my heart nearly split my chest open; or the way his soft full lips felt when they came to rest on mine. He gave a feather-light kiss at first gauging my response, and then settled on my mouth as if to be a weary traveler coming home. It was one of the most engulfing experiences I've ever had, before or since. My infatuation encompassed me completely and from that point on I did not question anything, logical or illogical, that Emmerick or Lucy said or asked of me. I loved Emmerick, and Lucy for that matter, so by the time Lucy asked me the nearly unthinkable, I was so in love that my hesitation was only momentarily noticed. Somewhere in the very, very back of my mind I had a 'proceed with caution' sign. But, it didn't say, 'don't proceed at all', right?

Chapter Ten

SEEING IS BELIEVING

I had gone from feeling like an ignorant child to feeling like a responsible and proactive woman of the world. It had been nearly three years since the first attack on Gdansk, Poland. I was still working at the 53rd squadron with Lucy and periodically corresponding with Brigitte to stay abreast of what news I could carry to Emmerick and Lucy. This was of course critical information that I passed on. I really didn't know a lot about what they did with the reports, but I was always reminded of what an irreplaceable position I held in our operation. There was an ugly war raging all around us, and I found myself feeling very self-important.... and mature. My relationship with Emmerick still mostly consisted of our weekly meetings, sometimes we had dinner which usually ended in his usual sweet good-night kiss. He was a very busy man, between trying to maintain the façade of an SS soldier and helping people steer clear of the work camps. So, although under normal circumstances one might have thought our relationship was moving at a snail's pace, these were not normal circumstances. I was very proud of myself for being mature enough to understand and accept that. I did have a little twinge of jealousy when I heard from Mother that Anneliese and Armin were engaged. Not because of any juvenile feelings for Armin that my mother thought I had, but because her life was now moving in the direction that my fantasies took me in daily. So, when a night came that Emmerick asked me to stay with Lucy for the weekend in order for us to take a day trip, I immediately said yes. I began conjuring all kinds of scenarios of our day date…maybe a romantic picnic…maybe taking us to his home…walking…holding hands…I could barely wait. An entire day and evening together! Could this be the day that he says the magic words? He surely had something special in mind to have me spend the weekend with Lucy.

This was not the "date" I had imagined though. Emmerick had been working with a group that transported supplies to Buchenwald, a work camp near Weimar. One of his old school mates worked as a watchtower guard there and he wanted to meet Lucy. When Emmerick described the upcoming day, my whole being deflated. This was really about some guy wanting to meet Lucy. I guess it was an opportune time for Emmerick and I to spend some time together…nevertheless, I was completely disappointed. Apparently, this other guy would be "working" and we would be going there to meet instead of him coming to us. I almost wanted to stamp my foot in protest, but that wouldn't match the mature lady I was. Emmerick had some kind of work to settle while we were there as well…. great…he would be working…Lucy would be flirting…. I suppose I would be sitting.

So, it was to be a working double date of sorts. It didn't occur to me at first that we might be going into the actual camp. I hesitantly asked if we would be going into the camp, and Emmerick said that we would. This was extremely surprising to me as I never imagined I would see a camp, nor did I want to. I asked how this could even be possible…to bring two women into the camp that aren't military. Apparently, it wasn't uncommon for women to be brought into the camps to the officers' quarters. So, it became clear to me that this is what we would be thought of…entertainment. None of this went along with my various date fantasies, and I let Lucy and Emmerick know that I was very uncomfortable and not at all sure I wanted to go.

"Lucy, this is craziness! I can't believe I'm the one having to say so! We don't even know what could happen if we were found out to be in the camp! I can't believe you are so agreeable to it! I can't…I just can't!" I continued my protests for several more hours first turning to Lucy, then to Emmerick. They of course said I didn't have to go at all…they suggested this would be an opportunity to see the working conditions that the Jews faced and what we were trying to save people from. But they more than understood if I just wasn't ready for something like that. I was also told that Lucy had been in one before and it was the catalyst that propelled her into her rescue mission. By the time these two were done with me, I was right back to feeling like a child. They could have sold snake oil to a snake! I didn't like it at all…but in the end…I agreed to go.

Emmerick picked us up early on a Saturday morning and we drove to Weimar. As we wound around the curved dirt road I could see the front gate attached to the walls of the entrance. A slogan had apparently been made as part of the gate, "Jedem das Seine…. everyone gets what they deserve." I couldn't believe that blatant statement! I felt my stomach twist and must have made some kind of noise or gasp because Emmerick turned to me and said, "Effie, you must not give us away! You have to appear to agree with them! You will be risking your life if you act otherwise. It doesn't bother them to throw non-Jewish Germans in there!"

All I could do was nod. What had I been thinking to come along? I really didn't want to see any of this!

Emmerick slowly approached the guard house and presented his credentials. The guard motioned toward Lucy and me and we handed over our naturalization papers. Emmerick then gave the guard some off-color explanation for bringing two young females to the camp. We drove into the camp, and had to pass through another gate attached to barbed wire fencing. We drove further up the path and I just sat looking out of my window. To the left were rows and rows of long buildings that looked like some type of barracks. Then to the right was a large brick building that had smoke coming out of the chimneys in evenly spaced puffs. A little way down the central path and to the left was another brick building that looked just like a factory. All around the perimeter there were two rows of barbed wire fencing with a walking path in between. SS soldiers were rounding the perimeter in that path. It appeared that there were four watchtowers at each corner of the camp and a densely-wooded area to the far end outside of the fence.

As if reading my mind, Emmerick gave us a verbal tour of the camp. The barracks were indeed just that, housing for the detainees. The bigger of the brick buildings was a munitions factory. Before he could finish telling us about the last building, an officer walking up the path waved Emmerick to a stop. Emmerick turned to Lucy, "This is him."

"Stephan, good to see you old friend!"

"Not nearly as old as you!"

The two laughed as if they had met at the market on a Sunday afternoon. Emmerick introduced Stephan and Lucy. "Emmerick, park over there – upwind so you won't smell the stench as much, then come with me. I will give you this week's supply list then we can catch up." Stephan directed Emmerick to park a little beyond the first brick building. We got out and started to walk between two smaller wooden buildings that Stephan said were admitting offices. As we rounded the corner at the upper end of the building, I stopped dead in my tracks. Walking on the opposite side of the road was a line of men, some in clothes and some not. There were officers at the beginning of the line and the end and one on each side. Emmerick and Stephan had been walking in front of me and Lucy, but that did nothing to obscure the view. These men…were…walking skeletons! No hair, practically no flesh, most were naked, they were beyond filthy and so extremely, painfully thin. They were walking slowly despite the raging of the front soldier. One man turned his face toward us, I saw him and I knew deep in my soul that he saw me. His face was dirty and unshaven and his eyes were sunken with purple encircling them. His mouth was dried and cracked, and that dark stain could have been dried blood, I wasn't sure. His eyes met mine and they accused and pleaded with me all at the same time. "Don't you see me? Don't you see that I'm human? Don't you see the pain I'm in, the fear that's in my heart? Don't you see the sorrow – the sorrow of knowing what they did to my wife…and I couldn't save her? Don't you see I was just like you, I'm a child of God too?!" His eyes screamed into mine, past my mind and into my soul. I wanted to run to him and hold him and scream and claw at the soldiers to release them! Oh God, my mind screamed, what have we done?!! I needed to run…but I stood. I stood there staring as they walked by. I only moved when Emmerick touched my arm, "Effie, did you hear me? We are going into Stephan's office." Then I turned from that tortured spirit, and walked away.

For the next hour, I was an automaton. I responded appropriately to all comments directed toward me. Finally, their business was done and we began our walk back to the car. "We will go this back way to the car. The wind has changed directions." Stephan said has he angled his position to be next to Lucy.

As if my whole being had not been shaken enough, I had to keep up the pretense of being one of them, of being the heartless monster that the prisoner saw. We reached the end of the back side of the building where there were wooden double doors that were slightly open. I shouldn't have looked, I had seen enough, but I was on that side of our group, closest to the door. The other three were in a conversation so I looked. There was an old mule cart with a tarp partially covering the contents. Legs normally didn't cause me to feel faint and force the rush of bile into my mouth – but this time they did. I gagged and doubled over barely far enough to miss myself as I heaved and blindly reached for the side of the building. Emmerick grabbed my arm and Stephan immediately saw what I had seen. "YOU IDIOTS!! SHUT THE DOORS, YOU ARE SUPPOSED TO KEEP THAT TRASH COVERED!" He continued to berate the soldiers as Lucy came to me and wrapped her arms around my waist and held me until I somehow managed to stop. We made our way to the car and I sat in the back seat with Emmerick's handkerchief to my mouth as tears rolled uncontrollably down my face.

I didn't have to ask what that building was. All I could say, indiscernible through my sobs, was an apology to that man – that man making his way to the crematorium, back to ashes and dust, back to God.

I had been profoundly put in my place the day we went to Buchenwald. All of my thoughts and actions up until this point had been solely for my ego, my sense of accomplishment. How unbelievably obtuse I had been! My focus had truly not been on helping anyone, but doing just enough to ease my conscience so I could pat myself on the back and still not be put in too hard of a situation. I also found myself wondering how Emmerick and Lucy had been able to experience the same atrocious scene without having a completely visceral response. I wondered how they or anyone could see those men, the walking dead with their skeletal frames and gaunt faces and even more…..the humans trapped inside; and not have any reaction at all. The shame and guilt I felt for standing still and watching the death march was nearly more than I could handle. I couldn't go to my parents for comfort, I couldn't go to my church…. I could go to God, but I was so angry with Him. I couldn't even talk to Emmerick or Lucy, yet. In my mind, I murdered him…them…with my silence. I was the same as the soldiers. It was their life or mine and I chose mine. And I was sickened by that choice.

Chapter Eleven

Summer 1942

German troops were moving in on Stalingrad in the late summer of 1942 and early part of 1943. In Wiesbaden, the spring and summer leading up to that fall was a kaleidoscope of events. The presence of SS soldiers around every corner was so much the norm it would have almost been a fearful thing had they suddenly disappeared. We had our regular air raid drills and blackout curfews as well as living on our rationing coupons, but even with all of this, as a German, life was not so very far removed from pre-war life. My father continued to go to work every day and my mother managed our home with the help of the only housekeeper we were able to keep. It was this summer that my grandmother became ill and my mother went to Frankfurt to stay with her some. Father would take the train on weekends to be with them. I stayed home with our housekeeper. It wasn't a summer that a young bride-to-be would have dreamed of, but weddings happened none the less. It was that summer that Anneliese and Armin had their wedding. It was a small affair, which I attended alone. I had been back on speaking terms with Emmerick after I met with him to at least try to understand his lack of reaction the day we went to the camp. He had given a convincing enough speech, but he was still working his way back into my good graces. I was the only one from my other group of "friends" who was able to attend. Brigitte had sent a gift and thankfully Sepp's outfit was in Munich. It was a melancholic event for me…a sad nostalgia of what once was and what seemed to be slipping further away. That world of parties, marriage, children…that seemed so far away from me and an impossible dream for the Jews was slowly being eclipsed by this dark new world void of normal joys.

I went through the appropriate motions of one attending a friend's wedding, smiled at key moments, laughed at the humorous wedding toast, and allowed mist to pool in my eyes when the moment dictated. My physical body was present, playing the part just like everyone else in this game of charades titled "a normal life". By the end of the evening, Armin was whisking Anne away for their honeymoon weekend and new home with him. What is it about weddings that makes one utterly desperate to be part of an 'us' and 'we'? I was not immune to the seemingly air-born romance virus floating around so I decided that maybe I should be gracious and reunite the couple of Effie and Emmerick.

I extended the olive branch to him, and before long we were back to weekly meetings with Lucy and dinners for just us. And though evidence of the war was as thick as the summer air all around us, and every now and again I was asked to be in contact with Brigitte and Anne, that was the closest summer to normal that I was to have. My mind and soul already bore scarring from the trip to Buchenwald and my body was soon to be scarred as the last treasure of youth would be ripped from me.

CHAPTER TWELVE

Present Day

Twilight is such a lovely peaceful time when one isn't worried about night bombing raids. It is a magical time when I love to do my best thinking. I am fortunate to still be able to think of things present…and past. I have been thinking about my afternoons with my sweet confidante Pam. I have been recounting my youth to her. She is so curious just like others her age. She has a romantic view of the war and the people who survived. And what I have told her so far has been harsh enough. I don't know what compelled me to tell her so much already, but I have decided to tie my story up with a neat pink ribbon that will make Pam smile instead of burdening her with the degrading truth. It's not her history nor should she be strapped with the knowledge of it. I am having trouble remembering why I started down this path with her except that she asked and I felt ready to tell. But now that such ugliness could come out, I no longer feel that I can share it with her. There is someone, two people actually, who should know the whole story. Just this thought alone causes me to have to take a deep breath as it is suffocating to think of actually saying out loud what has been. What would my level-headed husband have done? If he had lived I wonder if I would ever think of telling them. I sigh to myself as I wish for the millionth time that he was still here. Didn't he know I still needed his guidance? From the day we met, I don't think I ever made a decision without his sound advice. When I was a firecracker, he was a calming presence. When I was a blustering wind blowing through the house, he was the sweet-smelling refreshing air that put everything back right. Oh, he disciplined the children, but always in such a quiet way, it almost affected them more than my ranting and raving. I wasn't always in a foul mood; I just always wanted to protect the children, from everyone and everything. He would know just how to tell them all of this. I, on the other hand, would most likely just put it out there. I'm sure my life expectancy isn't as long as I or any of us would like and I wish that my last few years could be could be spent in truth, but this could be at the cost of their love and trust. Should they hear it from me before I take my exit? Well who else, silly old girl? You are the only one left that knows what a terribly wretched monster you are. Maybe not the last living member of the group, but the only one left with the true story.

So, twilight has helped me decide. I know my children will despise me. They may never forgive me, but there is the hope that they will come to understand. And they have a right and a need to know. I think it's time to go through my things at the house and tell them the story and give them what's theirs. Maybe I should rehearse this autobiography a few more times in my mind before they hear it. Maybe there's a way to soften the blow. I entertain thoughts that maybe I have blown this up so much in my mind that they might not react nearly as bad as I believe they will. Only one way to find out.

CHAPTER THIRTEEN

August 1942

Lucy and I weren't as close as I thought we would become before our trip to Buchenwald, but we were certainly still friends. I still ate lunch with her every day at work and went to her apartment often, especially with Mother still in Frankfurt and Father working. Father had met both Emmerick and Lucy and liked them. I was happy that Father had approved of Emmerick even though he wasn't Armin. And Emmerick and I were only dating after all. Emmerick was a perfect gentleman, sometimes irritatingly so. But, I had to always remember he had an awesome responsibility as a soldier, but more than that, to the Jews that he helped. There would be plenty of time for the traditional courting experience once this war ended, but for now the most important thing was staying in a position to help as many Jewish people as possible and we all three felt that way.

There was always restlessness in the air, but I could feel something more tense pressing down like the stale quiet air before a heat storm. Lucy and I even talked about it one day at lunch. It was another seemingly benign conversation that would have not so benign consequences.

"This weather is crazy this year isn't it Effie? One day the heat is unbearable, then the next the rain is so cold people are wearing overcoats." Lucy observed between bites of boiled egg.

"Mmmm. Nothing ever feels right anymore. Something is about to happen it feels like…. something near." Our conversations were never really about the weather. Lucy casually looked around at the other tables in the lunchroom before she spoke.

"There's going to be another roundup. This time straight from here to Theresienstadt. It's supposed to be at the end of the month. Mostly older

Jews, but there are still some younger ones here in the ghetto." Lucy spoke quietly with a smile on her face so that she appeared to be talking about nothing more important than her last date.

"Emmerick surely has something in mind? He hasn't mentioned anything to me, but I haven't seen him in several days. Have you talked to him about this?"

"Yes, he…. we…have something in mind. We know one of the families scheduled to go. We know their daughter; she was a friend of ours before all this. She's the one we are thinking of."

"What's her name?"

"Miriam Herskowitz." Lucy whispered her name as if speaking of some deity.

"Miriam Herskowitz." I repeated the name that would always, from that day on, be in the forefront of my mind. "What is the plan? Can you tell me anything about it?" I assumed I would be part of it, otherwise she would have never mentioned it.

"We have to hide her. That's it. We have to keep her hidden until we can get her to family in Zurich. She needs to be somewhere that she won't have to be seen for anything, not even to get food." The break whistle screamed the end of our lunch and our conversation.

"It's time to get back to work. Are we still having brunch at your house Sunday?" Lucy asked as she gathered her purse and lunch box.

"That's what I have been planning on. I'm guessing you want to wait until then to talk about this."

"Good girl." Lucy smiled and dropped her trash in the can.

I too discarded my trash and went back to work. So, that's our next mission, to save Miriam Herskowitz. What of the others? How many would be put on the train that day? I couldn't let those questions distract me though. We just have to do the best we can.

CHAPTER FOURTEEN

Miriam

That following Sunday Lucy and I had our now fairly regular Sunday brunch. We were all affected by using rationing coupons, but all in all, our family was very fortunate in the amount of food we had. We still had some vegetables, we were able to get some milk and butter at times. We also had plenty of eggs, so in comparison, we had plenty even if it wasn't nearly the feasts we used to have on Sundays. After our brunch, we took advantage of the decent weather and went for a walk around my families' grounds. We had often walked this area, but today we walked to the back of the garden where a small stream divided our property. In the left-hand corner of the garden there was a small arched wooden bridge that crossed the stream and led to the path to our barn and greenhouse. Lucy kept the conversation light as we reached the front of the barn. "Effie, are you a farm girl deep down?" Lucy laughed good-heartedly.

"No, actually this barn hasn't been used in a while, at least not since Father had to let our gardener go. It's mostly used to store garden tools and supplies for the greenhouse."

"Can we go in?"

"Sure, we can go in although there is not much to see."

I tugged on the plank that held the doors closed and then pulled the heavy wooden doors open. I took Lucy on the grand tour of the barn including the loft area. The loft was actually a closed off area only accessible by a ladder through a trap door. I laughed at all the oohing and ahhing coming from Lucy, but then her smile faded and she all at once turned serious.

"Effie, I think you know what I'm thinking. What about here? Why don't we hide Miriam here?"

"HERE???" I asked much more loudly than I anticipated. "You want me to hide her in here, in my father's barn? What if Father finds her? What if the soldiers do? Then what will happen to us?"

"What will happen to her if we don't? Effie, I'm not asking you to take this responsibility alone. Of course, Emmerick and I will help. I would never ask you if there were another place. Please Effie; she's such a dear person to us. It breaks my heart to just let her board that train." I could see the desperation in Lucy's face. My heart was torn as well, how could I possibly put my family in danger? But then that man's face was brought back to my mind…. that accusing look that made sure I knew I was just as guilty as the soldiers if I didn't help. How is it that we as humans can feel such guilt until an opportunity comes along to assuage that guilt and suddenly we move into self-preservation mode?

"Lucy, why hasn't Emmerick talked about this with me? And how can she go undetected here?" I fired random shots at her, mostly to stall before answering.

"Effie, Emmerick and I have known her for so long and he thought it would come better from me. And as far as keeping her hidden, this isn't the first time Emmerick has hidden people in order to get them to safety. Please say yes Effie! Isn't this what you wanted when we met at the café? Don't you remember how you felt at Buchenwald?" Lucy pleaded.

"Of course, I do! I can't believe you'd ask me that!" I was incensed! I turned from Lucy and leaned against the ladder that was propped on the wall. Hot tears of anger and petulance spilled down my cheeks. I wasn't insensitive, I did care! After several minutes of letting what I felt like were childish tears fall unchecked, I wiped my face and turned back to Lucy. I have to think about it…I need to consider all the consequences. This could literally be life or death for my family! There has to be somewhere else…surely Emmerick can find some other barn or building somewhere."

"Effie, I understand the risk you would be taking, I truly do…but if we don't move her soon she will be on that train at the end of the week. If we had enough time to find another place, we would. As it is, this could be her best maybe only chance to survive. Maybe we can find another place once we get her out of this round up this week. I give you my word, you will not be on your own through this. Please Effie!"

My heart was pricked by her pleading. I had never seen Miriam, but in my mind, I pictured a small framed young girl with hopes and dreams that may never be realized. Then I pictured the SS dragging me and my father and mother into the middle of the street and shooting us! The thing about youth is that young people generally have more of a 'nothing will happen to me' attitude than we do as adults. The young girl needing a chance at a future won the battle in my mind.

"We will bring her here. She will stay in the loft. Father doesn't come out here anymore and I will just have to trust Emmerick to keep any soldiers away. How soon can she be brought here? What will she need up in the loft?"

Lucy grabbed my shoulders and hugged me. "You are providing the place, I will bring the rest. We will all take turns bringing her food. I promise we will move her as soon as possible! Thank you, Effie!"

Of course, nothing is as easy as it sounds. Miriam would need more supplies than Lucy could bring, Emmerick was going to have to keep a close watch without drawing any attention to our home, and I was going to have to keep Father from finding her. Over the next couple of days, we worked as covertly as possible and as quickly as possible to have her moved before the next roundup. It was Emmerick's job to get Miriam out of the ghetto and to the barn. I waited in the loft that night for what seemed like an eternity and finally the small side door opposite of the house opened and I heard the faint sounds of the trio coming in. I took a deep breath and realized I was very nervous to meet this girl that I knew nothing about. I came to the edge of the loft and held up a dimly lit lantern. I had already hung the blackout cloth over the small round window facing the garden. Lucy climbed up first, followed by a small-framed girl (just as I had pictured) with glossy black hair. Emmerick steadied the ladder then followed. As Miriam topped the ladder, I was struck by her gaunt face and huge black eyes that gave her face neither a haunted look nor an ethereal look, but something in between. The second thing that struck me as she threw her leg over the last rung was her firmly rounded stomach. I'm sure my mouth fell completely open…the child was nearly ready to deliver, though I suppose I could hardly call her a child. I reached out to take her hand, and instead of taking my hand she grasped me and hugged me. "Thank you!! Thank you for saving our lives!! Mine and my baby's!!" She conveyed such gratitude in a soft, young, voice. "Um…of course… we will do all that we can." I released Miriam and we all worked quickly and quietly to get her settled into the loft that would be her home until Emmerick could get her safely to Zurich. I had already brought a loaf of bread, two hard-boiled eggs, a small wedge of Muenster cheese and water. She sat on the cot and wrapped her arms around her expanded middle. She placed her hand high on her stomach and smiled as she promised safety to her unborn child.

We all left the barn at different times, Lucy first, then me, and Emmerick left last constantly checking the surrounding yard. The three of us gathered at the kitchen entrance of my house and spoke in hushed voices about our next steps. I agreed to go to the loft in the mornings to take breakfast and water and towels. Lucy would take a couple of evenings and Emmerick would come by late at night or opposite evenings from Lucy. Of course, we wouldn't even know when the other was there to ensure as little attention as possible would be drawn to my house. With the basics covered, I broached the obvious.

"Why didn't either of you tell me she's pregnant? What do we do if she needs a doctor? Where's the father?" I fired one question after another.

"Effie, we knew you were taking a great risk to let Miriam come here…I didn't think you would be as willing to help if you knew…. I'm sorry." Lucy spoke but Emmerick looked from his left to his right as if watching for intruders and said nothing.

"She's not due for three to four more weeks, and we will be moving her by then. The father is not able to be with her now." Lucy seemed much more convinced of our abilities to move Miriam quickly than I felt.

"Emmerick, don't you have anything to say? I would think you both know me well enough to know I would do what I could to help. Not only are you pulling away from me, but you two are making decisions behind my back and only giving me half-truths to get what you want!" My eyes welled with angry tears as I spoke, partially from self-pity and partially from justified anger even though just a few hundred feet away there was a poor desperate soul just trying to survive. Emmerick looked down at his feet as they shuffled back and forth, his hands were in his jacket pockets.

He took a deep sigh before he spoke. "Effie, I can't thank you enough for being so kind and helpful in so many different ways. You've done everything we've asked and done them so bravely and unselfishly. I'm sorry it seems we've kept information from you, believe me, it's never been done to hurt you. You don't know how often I wish this was a different time that we were just two people that met and every time we were together was only just to get to know each other better and to date like a normal couple. You are very special and I only mean to protect you by keeping you from knowing too much." He held his hand out, palm up and I placed my hand in his. He raised it to his lips and kissed it. The pooled tears rolled over the bottom rim of my eyes and down my cheeks. Emmerick used the thumb of his other hand and wiped them from my face. "What we ask of you is hard, and I know that. Please, just a little more help and it will all be over." I nodded, as I didn't trust myself to speak. Emmerick wrapped his arm around my shoulders and kissed my temple. Lucy squeezed my arm and said she would see me at work the next day. I don't know how they thought I would sleep between now and the next morning, but she also admonished me to get some rest. I simply nodded, whispered a goodbye as I glanced back to the barn and went into my home.

Emmerick and Lucy crossed through the back yard and walked as quietly as their shadows through the yards and allies as to not draw attention to themselves. They reached the café parking where they had left Emmerick's car and as Emmerick opened the door for Lucy, he finally spoke. "When all of this is over, I will have to do something very special for her. She has been so brave and strong." Lucy gave him a sadly knowing smile, "If she's still with us after all this. I don't want to sound harsh, but you know the risks involved with what we are doing. But for all of you, and myself of course, I pray that we get Miriam to Zurich before she goes into labor and without anyone suspecting us. Will this be our last cause?"

"There is one more round-up planned for Wiesbaden. I will see if there's anything that we could do. After that, yes, we will then just be trying to survive until the end of this blasted war."

"Miriam will be forever grateful to you."

"Yes, well, it is the very least I can do."

Miriam lay perfectly still on her cot covered with layers of blankets.

Her eyes were accustomed enough to the scant light in the loft that she was able to look at her new, hopefully safe home. The walls were a worn grey with various gardening tools hanging neatly arranged. In the corner was an old milking can, the other corner had a large bucket for her necessary use. Her cot was padded with fresh straw that had a sweet, freshly cut smell. The blankets were clean and crisp with the night cold. She was so very thankful for God to have brought her to a safe place. Even in her sin, her God was watching over her and her child. The timing had just been all wrong. If the war wasn't going on, she and the love of her life could have married. That was still no excuse for her moment of weakness that now had her fighting for her life and the life of her unborn baby. Now, she would likely never be able to marry the father, all she can hope for is safety. Emmerick had worked tirelessly to help not only her, but many other Jews to safety. And Lucy, she had always been such a close friend, and still was. This new friend, Effie, must be truly special to hide her. She would say a special prayer for their safety. Miriam closed her eyes and fell into the most peaceful sleep she had known in quite a while.

Miriam woke the next morning and began the day much the same as she did every other, with her morning prayer. "Modeh ani l'faneykha, melech chai vekaiyam, shehechezarta bi nishmati bechemlah, rabbah emunatekha." (I thank you, living and eternal King, for returning my soul within me in compassion, great is your faithfulness.) As she finished her prayer, she felt someone stirring in the barn. She lowered her shawl and opened her eyes to see Effie coming over the top rung of the ladder through the trap door carrying a basket and small pitcher of water. "Good morning...I brought your breakfast and some towels. Did you sleep well?"

"Yes, very well, thank you Effie." Miriam smiled so graciously, one would hardly know the unimaginable predicament she was in. I felt so at odds with myself...happy to help Miriam, but terrified of the cost if we were caught. And I still could not shake the feeling of betrayal by Emmerick and Lucy. He seemed sincere with his apology last night, but something with me told me something was still amiss. The pieces just weren't fitting together. Nevertheless, I promised to help and I would.

"Well, anything I can do to help until you can get to Zurich. I'm on my way to work, but is there anything else you need? Remember, you MUST stay up here, I will be moving the ladder when I leave."

"You are being so wonderful; no, I don't need anything else at all. I can't thank you enough." Miriam looked at me with those huge black eyes and utmost trust. I can't explain why, at that moment, I felt jealousy.

Chapter Fifteen

Present Day

I watched Ruthie and Jonathon surreptitiously look around the house as if they were visiting a museum instead of standing in the home they were raised in. The day had come to pack up the house and tell my children our story. I had already made a written plan for my furniture and major appliances, so it really just came down to smaller more personal items that needed a new home. Since I had decided to do this, I had been extremely focused. When Pam came back from holiday we resumed our chats, but I never finished. I told her about Miriam, except the ending I gave Pam was the version that Emmerick came late one night and whisked Miriam away, heroically, to her family in Zurich. I gave her the generic edition of the rest of the war. I told her, "So you see Pam, nothing as romantic and outstanding as you wanted to believe." Pam declared me a saint for helping Miriam and the others. I said I was no such thing, and we moved back into our resident/caregiver roles. And so, that just left telling the real version to my children.

"Jonathon, Ruthie let's start in my room. I have some things that Ruthie discovered that I want to give you that I saved from the war." My children followed me to my bedroom and I opened the middle drawer of my desk. I also opened the chest at the foot of my bed. Inside were quilts, jewelry, letters, baby clothes, pictures and a couple of smaller boxes. It was the content of the crystal box that my children needed to see, had a right to see along with an explanation. I pulled them completely out of the desk and sat them on my bed. I motioned for Ruth and Jonathon to take a seat in the pair of wing-backed chairs in front of the window. I sat on the edge of the bed and laid my hand on the box maybe to buy myself a moment or two or maybe to calm my nerves. "I have some pretty special things in this box and chest for the two of you, but before I give them to you, I need to tell you how it happened that they came to be in my possession. As you both know, in 1939 I was seventeen years old…."

CHAPTER SIXTEEN

1942

"Effie!!! It's so good to see you again!!" My mouth apparently forgot that it was rude to stand agape without any sound coming out, but as I looked at my two old friends I couldn't seem to make it do anything else. I was spared from speaking by Brigitte and Anneliese taking turns grabbing and hugging me. I was completely stunned to have walked into the sitting room to find my two old friends waiting on me. "I can't believe you're here!" was about all I could mutter. I was to receive the explanation that Brigitte had a long weekend and surprisingly Anneliese was back in town with Armin who had to come back for some assignment. The two girls had corresponded and decided to meet up while they were here and come surprise me. Surprise was definitely one of the emotions I felt, along with a feeling of defensiveness and panic. I was harboring a Jew for Heaven's sake! And not only that we were on opposite sides of this war, only they didn't know it! Then there was this feeling of being cornered…. why all of a sudden were they here…right after moving Miriam in? I no longer trusted the motives of my oldest friends, but I had to pull off an incredible impersonation of the old Effie. "I'm ecstatic!! I can't believe you are here! How long will you be home?" I forced my shaking hands to be still by folding them on my lap and plastered a huge smile on my face.

Anne was the first to speak, "Well, Armin is here for some assignment for this week so I will be here until he's finished, but I believe Brigitte goes back to Ravensbruck tomorrow."

"Yes, I only rode in on a semi-holiday, but I will be going back to the clinic tomorrow. Effie, I have so appreciated your letters! You should come to Berlin with me; you have shown so much interest in what we are doing."

"Well, you know Father's thoughts on me leaving. And I feel that I've been doing a little part by working with the Luftwaffe, of course nothing close to your…. contribution."

"Don't be silly! Every German does their part and more!" Our conversation turned to more benign topics, and for a split-second I relaxed and felt a twinge of the old camaraderie from our youth. The visit ended nearly as abruptly as it began when Armin showed up at the front door to collect Brigitte and Anne. Just like the last time I saw Armin, there was little conversation. I walked them to the door and looked out to see Sepp propped up next to the car smoking a cigarette. I must have looked surprised because Armin looked at me sharply and asked if anything was wrong. "You recognize Sepp, don't you?"

"Of course, I do…. it's just been a surprising day to see everyone from our old group." Sepp looked up at me and slightly inclined his head. So, either Armin was truly confused or Sepp had poisoned him against me with his version of what had happened. Either way, I just wanted this little reunion to end. I told my company goodbye once more and stepped back into the house. I was supposed to check on Miriam this morning, but there was no way I was going close to the barn today. I decided this was something that Lucy and Emmerick needed to be aware of so I waited just long enough for the foursome to be well up the road before climbing on my bicycle and headed straight to Lucy's apartment. I took my usual route, through the town, past the church parallel to the train station. While there was always the military presence, it seemed that there was a heavier concentration at the train station. I would have normally allowed curiosity to slow me down but I felt pushed to reach Lucy's.

Out of breath, I reached Lucy's apartment, darted up the steps and buzzed her number. The door opened and Lucy pulled me in. "My goodness Effie, you're out of breath, what's wrong?" Lucy continued to pull me by the hand to a stool in her kitchen where she motioned for me to sit.

"Something very strange happened this morning." I reached for the glass of water she was handing me.

"What? What happened?"

"I had visitors, my old friends, Brigitte and Anneliese. Before I could barely contain my surprise, Armin and Sepp showed up to collect them." I briefed her with the condensed version.

"What did they say? Try to think of everything."

"Not much really, Brigitte said she had a weekend furlough and Anne had accompanied Armin here supposedly for some assignment he has here this week."

"I see. Did they say anything at all that led you to believe they knew about your guest?"

"No, but it's too much of a coincidence, don't you think?" I took several more drinks of water.

"Probably. Do you think you will see them again? We are going to have to make sure they don't suspect a thing about Miriam. It's better if you don't go to the barn, they may be watching you, but they won't know to watch me. I'll take care of her at night until they leave. Listen, Effie, you need to stick to work and home for the next couple of days. Are you ok?"

"Yes, just very surprised, shocked actually. I didn't check on Miriam this morning, I was afraid they were still too close by. But I'm sure she must be scared or worried. And she must be hungry, I hate for her to wonder why I haven't been out to take care of her." I truly was concerned about this young girl who was depending on us to live.

"Miriam has been hiding out for quite awhile. She knows to expect changes in routine. Don't worry; the most important thing is to not lead anyone to her."

I stayed at Lucy's long enough to catch my breath and calm down. We talked a little more about my visitors, work, Emmerick, and how the war had inexplicably changed all of us and our lives. We talked about what we would be doing now if the war hadn't happened. I told her I liked to imagine me and Emmerick dating like normal people, going to movies and dinner. Lucy responded to my confession that she guessed that was one good product of the war, me meeting Emmerick, surely just as our lives would have been different, his would have been very different too.

I finished my water and left. I rode back the same way I came and could barely get beyond the railway station with all the soldiers running about. There was shouting and hammering and soldiers unrolling barbed wire fencing. It was loud with a hurried, panicked atmosphere. They were building some type of pen across the tracks between two brick buildings.

It looked to be the space where a building used to stand. I slowed down just long enough to be nearly knocked over by soldiers carrying boards toward the empty lot. I moved on toward home feeling as though I had just found an elusive piece of a puzzle, but still couldn't place it in the picture.

CHAPTER SEVENTEEN

Gone is childhood

True to our agreement, I stayed away from the barn for the next couple of days. I hoped and prayed that Lucy was tending to Miriam. I went to work, came home, ate dinner, listened to the radio news and repeated the ritual over for the next few days until I thought I would go mad. I had not heard from my "friends" since their arrival and I hoped that they were gone. On the morning of the fourth day, I decided to take a chance and make a trip to town and see if I could arrange a meeting with Emmerick or Lucy. Before I left, my momentary bravery or stupidity lead me to the kitchen to load up a basket of fresh bread, boiled eggs, and a canister of milk. I covered these with a large napkin and stopped on the back porch to lay garden gloves and a hand spade and shovel on top of the contents. I slipped on the rubber boots that lived on the back steps and casually made my way to the garden at the front of our barn. I put on the gloves and made quite a show of pulling weeds and mounding dirt around the plants. I picked up the watering can at the barn door, took it to the pump and partially filled it. After watering the plants, I stood and looked at my work as I listened for any rustling leaves, footsteps…anything that would alert me to go back to the house. All I could hear was the sound of my own heart and shaky breath coming out of my mouth. I wiped my hands on my apron, put my gloves and tools in the basket and walked into the barn. It was eerily quiet and it smelled of damp, stale hay. There were no movements, nothing had been disturbed. I quickly looked around and decided the less time I spent in the barn, the better. I slid the ladder over to the loft and quietly but quickly climbed to the top. I looked over the top rail and saw that Miriam was laying on the cot with huge eyes staring back at me. I placed my finger to my lips to keep her silent, and I carried the basket over to her. Her eyes watched my every move. Once I was close enough, I could see how pale and pasty her face was.

"Miriam…how are you feeling? Has Lucy been here?" She nodded yes to my second question and replied "I think it may be close now. My back is burning and throbbing. It comes in waves."

"Did you tell Lucy? Is she arranging for a doctor?"

Miriam replied with an air of one pitying a small child. "Effie, doctors are not possible. This I will have to do on my own. If you or Lucy is here to help…I will be thankful…but it may happen when I'm alone. It just has to be. I will pray, God will hear me…"

"Miriam, I will come stay through the night, I will find a way to be here."

Miriam continued as if she hadn't heard me. "Effie, there's something you can do for me…I've lost so much, but I still have these…" She breathed words between holding her breath for several seconds at a time. She motioned to her prayer book and prayer shawl along with a small stack of what was left of her earthly possessions. "If you have to hide my baby, if they find me after it's born, please tell him how much I love him, and please give him these small gifts. Tell him his father was so very brave and loved him too. Will you do that Effie?" I pulled Miriam's hand into my own and placed my other hand on her forehead. "Miriam, don't be silly, you won't be separated! Emmerick is going to get you to Zurich! You and your baby!"

She smiled a ghost of a smile, a look of resignation and maturity overcame her face. "Yes, I'm sure he will do everything in his power to save us."

I wasn't sure what to say to comfort her; she seemed certain she would be separated from her baby. But I was certain Emmerick wouldn't let that happen. I was also certain I had been in the barn for too long so I tried to make Miriam more comfortable, I rubbed her back, wiped her face and placed the basket right next to her. I promised her I would find someone I could trust to help and come back and see her through this.

I scrambled down the ladder and only slowed my pace once I was outside of the barn. I walked as casually as I could through the garden, back to the house. I slipped off my rubber boots and went back into my house. I had to get to town as fast as possible, but couldn't risk anyone seeing me in a panicked state. I went to the trouble of putting on my gloves and hat so as to look as normal as possible. We had extra Franzbrotchan and honey so I tied some in a tea cloth as my pretense for bicycling to Lucy's. I left the house in as unhurried manner as possible. As I pedaled toward town a thought, more like a desire to see Emmerick first overcame me. I knew I could most likely find him working around the base and since I always carried my identification papers and work pass, I took the chance on making a show of taking food to my boyfriend. He could have some contact with someone with medical knowledge. All I knew was that I felt he would have the right answer. Fate must have intervened because as I was riding toward the base, a line of cars coming from the base passed me and I caught a glimpse of Emmerick driving one of the last ones. I waved not knowing if he would stop, but he did. He pulled to the side and stepped out of the car. He bent and gave me a quick kiss on my cheek in greeting and pulled out a cigarette and lit it.

"Effie, what brings you this way on your day off?" He spoke quickly and I could see a nervous twitch about his mouth.

"I was hoping to see you, I have rolls." I replied weakly.

Emmerick lowered his voice, "You should not be in town today. There's a lot going on. You would be better to go back home." Emmerick looked to his left at a few cars pulling around his slowly. He gave a loud laugh and patted my cheek as if I had said something endearing. I realized, of course, it was for the benefit of the other SS meandering around.

"One of my friends is feeling really bad. I thought about seeing if Lucy had something to make her feel better. Unless you know someone..."

Emmerick searched my face. He had a look on his face that said he understood but at the same time became very pale, especially around his mouth. He looked afraid. "Well, I won't keep you. I don't know of anyone else who could be helpful right now. Get Lucy to your friend by all means. And don't come back to town, at least not for a day or two. I think the best place for you is with your friend. She obviously needs someone with her. Go on now, ride to Lucy's then go straight home. I will call on you when I can, do you understand?" He was trying to recover a mask of light-hearted conversation. He gave me another quick hug and kiss and climbed back into his car. I got back on my bicycle and started to go to Lucy's by a short cut down a dirt road through the woods that skirted the edge of town.

What I didn't see was the black car that pulled out of line, and chose my same path.

I have often heard that when someone experiences a traumatic event, it is replayed, relived in slow motion detail so that every smell, every sound, every feeling is magnified and amplified until it's all one can see and hear. There's counseling for it, medicine for it, to make it quieter and less visible, unless you deserve to hear it and see it…everyday…for the rest of your life. I was in such a hurry to get to Lucy to get help for Miriam, I don't recall hearing a car door. The first sound I do recall was the sound of heavy slow footsteps grinding dried leaves into the dirt and the echo of brittle twigs crisply snapping in half. The hair on the back of my neck stood on end as my heart became even more accelerated….it could just be an animal…I decided to lay my paranoia at rest and chance a quick look behind me. A stupid mistake as my bicycle dove front-tire first into a small furrow carved out by rain, nearly sending me over the top of my handle bars. I wish I had gone over the handle bars instead of being slammed in the gut by them, knocking me off my bike as well as knocking every bit of air out of me. I landed on my hands and knees as my mouth smacked the frame of the wrecked bike. The pain burned from my mouth and up through my nose and I could taste the metallic flavor of blood and bicycle. Dazed, I must have temporarily forgotten about the footsteps…until a large leather-gloved hand grabbed my hair and jerked my head backwards. My arms were waving wildly trying to make contact and I was spitting blood as I yelled for this predator to stop, to leave me alone! Just then a second gloved hand crushed my already bruised and swelling face. My screams were muted, the woods were spinning as I was pushed and pulled. I scratched at the dirt floor under me and pushed until I was half turned. I saw the uniformed arm, the shiny black boot, the cap on the ground bearing the skull, and slowly…. the back of the gloved hand raising high above my head and then I heard the sound of the hit before I felt it. My face was ground into the dirt, filling my mouth creating a bloody paste that threatened to close my airway. I can remember the feel of the rough uniform scraping the inside of my thighs, I can remember the feel of the rocks and hard packed dirt under my stomach as he pressed hard down on my back. I can still feel the cool breeze blowing across the sides of my legs and lower back as my dress was pushed higher up. Then there was the searing and ripping at my core that coupled with the guttural howl of a trapped animal. I can remember the rhythm of his breathing, the slow build to a rapid decline, every sound that he made is stuck in my head like a hated song. When he was finished, he lay there, heavy and sweating on me. He laid his head close to my right ear, "You're not worth what you think you are to him, and now you're worth even less!"

After what seemed like an eternity he pushed off of me, but the weight was still there. The weight of shame, of something dead. I didn't move. I didn't scream. He straightened his clothes. He told me it was a shame I had such a terrible bicycle wreck. He told me not to bother saying anything, nobody would believe me, he was untouchable.

Of course, I knew who it was, I knew when I had turned sideways on the ground and he did nothing to hide it, he didn't have to. He was whistling as he strolled away. I lay still and waited…I don't know what for…perhaps I thought…. hoped…. I was dying. How could God…. where was He…did I make this happen? What was I supposed to do right now? Was I supposed to continue to lay here crying? I shifted to my side and drew my legs up and cradled myself. I was ruined.

CHAPTER EIGHTEEN

One more round up

The drizzle of rain did nothing to slow the buzz of activity at the train station. The cacophony of soldiers' shouts, steam coming out from under the train, the questions and cries of the large group of Jews corralled between two buildings…the rain muted none of it. The soldiers would soon start lining the Jews up to board the train. They stood huddled as close to the brick wall at the back of the make-shift pen as possible. They stood wearing suits and dresses, coats and hats and tags identifying them as the Jews appointed to go to Theresienstadt. They held their suitcases as if they expected to need these belongings once they reached their detainment camp. Emmerick felt the all too familiar knot in his stomach as the anticipated time drew closer to pull Miriam's parents out of the group. This would be his last attempt to aid any of the Jews, not because he didn't want to, but he could feel, he knew he was under closer scrutiny than he liked. The plan was fine…it might take a little longer to move them since Lucy would now be at Effie's helping with Miriam. Emmerick walked the area, working alongside the other officers in preparation for the move. The plan was simple, feign suspicion of the couple, accuse them of hiding other Jews in their home and demand they show him where or be shot. This round-up wasn't as heavily manned as the groups bound for Auschwitz so it should go smoothly. Plus, Emmerick worked with these soldiers so they wouldn't question him. Emmerick was thinking along these lines when a familiar figure walked on the opposite side of the train station. What on earth was Lucy still doing in town? Emmerick quickly made his way across the station, dodging soldiers and white streams of steam.

"Lucy…. what are you doing here? Why aren't you at Effie's?"

"What do you mean? I'm SUPPOSED to be here!"

"Effie was on her way to get you. Her friend isn't feeling well…she thought you could help."

"She never came to my apartment…what do you need me to do?"

Emmerick looked around and rubbed his hand through his hair. "You need to just go help Effie. I can handle everything down here as long as I can get to the attic in your apartment. Go to your apartment, make sure I can quickly get them into it, get anything you might need for Miriam and get on out to Effie's house. But do it carefully! Most of the guys are down here at the station to make sure this last group gets on the train, but you never know when a soldier is just around the corner." Emmerick placed his hand on Lucy's shoulder and squeezed. "Please, be very careful…. we just need to finish this one rescue."

Lucy circled through the station and went out the opposite end. She had a terrible feeling that something wouldn't go right this time…there was too much happening all at once…Miriam's baby, Emmerick trying to save her parents…such great risks were being taken. Lucy should have been more aware of her surroundings. She rushed up the steps and switched on the light to the kitchen, pulled the string hanging from the small square in the ceiling and let the attached ladder slide out. She ran to her bedroom and gathered string, scissors, towels and crammed them in a bag. Effie would surely have access to anything else they might need. She stopped at her bedroom door and turned to take one more, quick glance back to make sure she wasn't forgetting anything, and that's when she heard it…. the barely audible yet deafening "click" … "You won't be going anywhere tonight. Turned quite the little traitor, haven't you?"

Lucy had known this day would come. She knew that by making the choice to help Jews, she would sacrifice part or all of her life. Even now, even at what she felt sure was the end; she had to make one last sacrifice. She would have to steer this officer away from Miriam…otherwise Emmerick would be found out…the baby and mother could be killed. Emmerick and Lucy had practiced the plan if either of them were caught. They had a scape-goat to point to…they had gleaned enough information from Effie about her friends Anneliese and Armin to weave a tale linking them to their own crimes rather than ever point towards the hiding spot of Miriam.

Lucy delivered the practiced story in a halting way as if the information was being torn from her.

"Bravo…. nicely rehearsed story. It's a shame, though, that you wasted your last breaths reciting such a lie. You see, Armin Mueller is a friend of mine." The ice-cold voice of the soldier spoke the last words Lucy thought she might ever hear on this earth.

I had stayed curled in the fetal position for what seemed an eternity. Resigned that I was going to live….and live with this horrible sin that had been committed against me…. I remembered somewhere fluttering around the edges of my mind that Miriam was in labor; that I had been on my way to help her. I didn't even know how long I had been gone, but there was no way I could go to Lucy's now. I had to find the will and strength to put this horrifying day into a closed box and get back to Miriam. Somehow, I made my legs work and I stood, used my torn underclothes to wipe myself as clean as possible. I pulled my bicycle up and started pushing it toward home. I had lived in the country long enough to witness enough natural births to help her. She needed me…and that's what I would have to hold on to, to continue to move my feet forward. My bicycle rolled over the same dead leaves and broken twigs that just a short moment before had tried to be a warning to me. I alternately walked/ran and stopped to cry. I also continually looked behind me, I should've known he wouldn't be there. He already accomplished what he set out to do. I had wanted to cross the threshold into adulthood, but I had been pushed and shoved into it…and now something that I had thought about and anticipated to be an exciting and loving experience was now a disgusting nightmare. Instead of being filled with awe and wonder and delight, I had been filled with his horrific male essence…he was still in me and with me….and I would never be free.

Somehow, I made it back home, back to the barn. My shaking and badly scraped and bruised legs carried me up the ladder. I made my way to her cot. Her black hair was plastered to her dripping wet, pale face. Sweat was running from her forehead down her cheeks and off the tip of her nose. She had buried her teeth into her bottom lip until it bled. Her blanket was twisted around the bottom of her legs dampened by the rush of fluid that had left her body hours ago. Her gown was pushed up above her hips and it too was soaked with blood and water. Her breathing came out as sporadic gasps and puffs spaced apart by her holding it in as her bloodshot eyes squeezed shut and the external earth stopped spinning to allow the internal gripping and tearing to do its job until the invisible hands released her for fewer and fewer seconds before the next contraction rolled over her. By the time I returned home and gathered up everything I thought I might need, Miriam was already deep in the throes of labor. I kneeled in the straw next to Miriam. She was nearly past the point of being able to recognize that anyone was there. Between gasps of air, Miriam panted that she had to push. She raised her knees with some strength that I could not believe she still had, she grabbed her knees as I tried to put a wooden spoon between her teeth. Even in her tumultuous state, something in Miriam must have remembered the need for quiet and safety and she bit down on the spoon to keep from screaming. She pulled up toward her gripped knees and bore down. Her instincts took over and without any words of coaching, alternately bore down to help her body do what it already knew to do. Though she barely made a sound, I could have sworn her body groaned in its own protest to being distorted, its own hips being pulled apart, its own core now rejecting its once welcomed guest. The contracting paused just long enough that her body begged for another grip, one more push, to be delivered of this beautiful torment.

I tried to hold her up as she pushed, I wiped the pouring sweat from her face, and I whispered encouragement, though I don't know if she heard it. The minutes slipped into an hour then longer. I propped two rolled blankets and hay behind her back for support and changed my position to prepare for the little ones' entrance. Finally, a rounded mass of dark hair arrived. With just another few pushes from Miriam, a red, wet scrunched up face appeared and I immediately cleared the mouth. A disproportioned little pink body followed covered in its sticky white coating, Miriam cried silently, but her pains weren't over.

By the time the miraculous had occurred and Miriam was cleansed again and resting and I had discarded the bloodied sheets and gown, I entered my home a much older person than I was the day before. Thankfully, it was just me and our in-residence housekeeper at home. I was able to soak in a hot bath without waking anyone. I wanted to wash away Miriam's blood and sweat, I wanted to wash away the sweat and smell of my attacker, I wanted to cleanse my scraped, bruised knees and minister to the cuts on my lips and forehead. I wanted to scrub away the existence of the girl that survived the last twenty-four hours. I slipped underneath the water and held my breath debating on whether to stay under or allow myself to come out baptized to a new life; a life without innocence or joy or hope. As the bubbles rose to the top, I imagined every foul and dirty deed leaving me and floating above me like a barrier I would have to rise up through to live.

Emmerick's plan had failed. He had over-estimated his relationship with the other soldiers. His attempt to separate Miriam's parents under the guise of questioning them only accomplished a more expedient death for them and a round of questioning for him. It was over, his attempts to do any good. His life could just as quickly be over. He knew he would be followed, but he had to find a way to warn Lucy and Effie and make sure Miriam made it to safety. He may never see them again, that may be the safest way. The plan to move Miriam was already in place; Lucy knew exactly what to do should he become detained. As he left the office after his interrogation, he knew he had not convinced anyone of anything, but possibly bought himself enough time to defect. He was mentally preparing himself for leaving Germany when he heard a truck pull up along side of him. "Well, well…who do we have here? My old friend Emmerick! Where are you heading? Let me give you a lift." The soldier had been following Emmerick and keeping tabs on him for quite some time. All of his visits to his camp and their meetings here were leading up to this. There was enough suspicion of Emmerick to detain him, question him or even get rid of him without any eyebrows being raised. This could even lead to some recognition from his commandant.

Emmerick stopped and felt the color drain from his face. He only half-turned, half raised his hand in a "thanks but no thanks" motion. "Please, I insist. Surely you aren't heading to your little friend's apartment, such a pity, such a looker, those eyes and lips…and those legs! It will be a waste of time for you to go there. Emmerick…. get in the truck…old friend."

The ray of sun slowly climbed over the window seal, slanted across the coverlet and slowly traveled up the light peach colored wall. I could hardly believe the sun had the nerve to come up. Had someone forgotten to inform this symbol of hope and joy that its services were no longer needed? I could feel myself physically sinking further down into my mattress, wishing I could disappear into it and not have to face another day. My throat was raw from crying and my eyes felt like they had been scraped with sand-paper. I was living in a nightmare…it seemed like just yesterday the worst thing to happen would be not having a new gown to our next dance and now…I was involved with an SS soldier who delivered Jews to safety, I was myself harboring a young, newly mothered Jewish girl and as of yesterday, my one gift to offer my future husband had been stolen by a brutal thief. I was broken and ruined. I felt empty and desolate. I had been in church all of my life, and even now thought I was doing my Christian duty by caring for Miriam and yet…here I was…. I could not even call on God for the amount of anger I had towards Him. I wanted my mother, but I didn't want my mother. I wanted to get up and forget all of it, but I wanted to stay in bed forever. I wanted Emmerick to come and take Miriam to Zurich and come back to me, but I never wanted to see another male in that way again. Looking back now, I know even in that despair God heard me because somehow, I pushed the covers back, put my feet on the floor, got dressed, and prepared to help Miriam through her first day of motherhood. I would need to let Lucy and Emmerick know Miriam had delivered, and find out what the next step was in moving her.

I couldn't eat; I drank a cup of weak tea with a sparse amount of sugar. I again waited for our housekeeper to leave the kitchen and I packed up my breakfast for Miriam. And right at that moment I felt resentment toward her. I felt resentment toward her for needing help, for being Jewish, for having found a true love and bearing the fruit of that love. I resented the day I ever met Lucy or Emmerick. I resented my own country and fuehrer for destroying life, destroying Jewish lives, and I resented my own people for setting back and allowing all of this to happen! I was a bundle of emotions and thoughts. As quickly as I resented Miriam, my heart went out to her.

I climbed up the ladder into the loft and saw the new mother lying on her side looking down at the bundle next to her. She had such a glow of love on her face. "Guten morgan Effie! God bless you for helping us last night! Have you ever seen such beauty?" Miriam radiated with such love I humorously thought I should make sure the black-out curtain was completely drawn. I couldn't believe the transformation from labor to this. "I really didn't do anything Miriam; I do believe you did all the work!" I couldn't help but smile as her bundle of blankets moved and squirmed and began demanding breakfast too.

I stayed in the barn only as long as it took to help Miriam as she nursed and cleaned herself up. The small little family was already nestled back on the cot and nearly asleep by the time I climbed back down the ladder. As conflicted as I was in my feelings, one thing I knew for sure was that if she were to survive she needed to be moved and moved quickly. I was not at all sure how safe it would be to try to find a ride into town, but Lucy had not been out to the house for some time and I needed to let her know that time was getting away from us.

After dressing to go into town I walked into the kitchen to see our housekeeper reading the morning news. "I hope you aren't going in to town today Ms. Effie. They had quite a time with the round-up yesterday. It seems they are still looking for some unaccounted older Jews. Anyway, I believe your father will be home later this afternoon. It might be best to wait on him, or I can call my brother to bring anything out that you need." Our housekeeper talked as she read the paper shaking her head.

"I was actually going to check on a co-worker, a friend actually. I'm afraid she's not been feeling well and she really doesn't have anyone else to take care of her. I was thinking I might take some of your bread and soup to her…it has always worked wonders with me." I spoke confidently and firmly, and tried to stroke her vanity a little so I wouldn't raise any suspicion.

"Well, at least don't ride that bicycle of yours! It doesn't look fit to ride after your wreck anyway. And are you sure your lip is ok?" She had noticed my lip and forehead this morning. And true to my attackers' prediction, it was all due to my bicycle wreck.

"Yes, I'm fine, really. Mr. Wilhelm usually goes to work around this time; I will try to catch a ride with him. If he can't I will be right back in. Now, how about some of your bread?" I smiled and started gathering up a canister to put her soup in. Now that I knew my father was coming home I would have to get to town and back quickly.

As my neighbor and I rode through town and rounded the train station, I noticed at the end of one of the platforms there was a mounded pile of coats, suitcases, shopping bags, and shoes. I knew this had to be where the Jewish people from Wiesbaden had been placed on the trains, but why were there so many coats and shoes left? I asked my neighbor as much to which he replied, "Hmpff! Most likely those cheap Goldie-campers tried to escape! Looks like our boys rounded them up properly though!" My mouth was open and I just looked at him. "What??" he grunted and turned to look out the windshield. He pulled over where I asked him to drop me off. "Well, here you are. I will be here all day, if you are still in town I can give you a ride back." I quickly weighed my options, walk home or sit next to this Hitler-created monster. "My friend may be able to arrange a ride for me. Thanks though." He shrugged as I got out of the car. As I walked past the first two apartment buildings I was amazed to see normal routines continuing in the middle of this war, one day after a mass round-up of innocents or worse, and women were still beating out rugs and sweeping steps, men were still in coats and hats carrying sachet cases to work…. completely oblivious to the tragedies around them. I walked up the cobble stone street and turned right behind the bakery and crossed over one more street. Lucy had to make a move today. We were to be back to work the next day and with my father coming home, we had to either find a new hiding place or continue with the plan, but quickly. I so longed to get this over and to see the end of this war! I wanted to feel safe again, go out with friends, enjoy dressing up for…well…I couldn't really think what for. Who was going to marry me now? Emmerick? At times, I disliked him as much as I liked him. These thoughts accompanied me up the street and steps to Lucy's apartment. As I climbed the wooden steps inside Lucy's apartment building, I wondered if I could tell her about my attacker. I didn't want to think about it…much less talk about it, but what if something was still to come of it? What if I had become pregnant? I was so engrossed in my thoughts it took a few seconds to realize that Lucy's door was cracked open. I was brought abruptly back to where I was and what I was doing there and immediately felt on alert. I quietly pushed the door open and listened for a minute before calling out Lucy's name. No response came so I walked through her living room as my eyes darted over the room. I noticed newspapers lying on the couch, a tea cup still on the coffee table half full of tea. On the back of one chair was a scarf and next to the chair were a pair of Lucy's black wedge heels. I stepped into her kitchen and noticed her black purse carelessly sitting on the floor. Something was definitely off…Lucy was by no means a neat person, but she wasn't careless with her stuff. There was only one room left in her apartment, and I stood still, trying to talk myself into and out of looking in her bedroom. I could back out and go home, but what if she were sick in there? Maybe she needed me! But then again, what if she wasn't alone in there? What if someone was in there waiting on me to come around the corner? My hands were cold and yet I could feel tiny beads of sweat forming on my lip and forehead. My heart started beating faster and faster as I convinced myself I was about to walk into another attack! I slowly made me way down the very short hall and ever so cautiously looked through the crack between the door and the frame. I couldn't register the section of scene that was before me. I pushed her door open and stood staring. What on earth had happened in here? To say there had been a struggle in the room would have been a gross understatement…the bed covers were twisted and pulled and knotted, half on the bed, half off… the mattress was pulled half off of the bed frame…the curtains were barely hanging by the rod that was pulled out of one side of the wall….I looked further and saw that her dresser drawers were pulled out and clothes were strewn all over the floor….the bottles of perfume were turned over…her make-up was open and dripping on the top of her dresser…her tube of red lipstick was twisted all the way open….I turned to see something on her bathroom door…it too was as dark red as her lipstick but on a closer look it was splatters…it was splatters of sticky blood!! Not a lot…. but I knew somebody had hurt her…possibly raped her or worse!!! I looked down and right where I was standing was a dark circle in the already dark carpet. I knew before I bent down, but we have to always prove ourselves right or wrong…we can't just believe what we see. Sure enough, I had stepped in and now had laid my hand in a cold sticky puddle of blood!! My first reaction was to heave… but then suddenly I thought…maybe it wasn't her blood! Maybe she had been attacked but was able to fight back…I was pretty sure Lucy owned a hand gun…. maybe she had fought back and then Emmerick came to help her! Maybe they are heading to my house for safety!! My brain wanted to protect my heart and soul by creating this explanation. There wasn't a body here…it could be true! Even as my brain worked furiously to create more details to convince me that it was a true version, that Lucy had managed to escape…cold reality was there to contradict my poor mind. I didn't know the truth, I didn't know what happened to her, but something terrible had. Someone had caught up to her and now who knows what they had done to her. But, if someone found out about her…Miriam! I had to get out of here…. I was no help to Lucy here and even less help to Miriam!! I felt that I couldn't just leave though…. I wiped my hands off on a discarded towel lying in the bathroom floor and walked over to her dresser. Somebody had hurt my friend and left her few belongings just torn and pulled apart and laying around. I touched her hairbrush, her hand mirror; I closed her lipstick and put it in my pocket. I wanted to scoop up all her belongings and put them in a safe place for her for when she came back. Just as I was about to walk away, I took one more glance back at her dresser and at the beveled mirror above it. My ragged reflection was not what had caught my eye, but a small sliver of white paper sticking out from behind the mirror. How odd for something so small in such a big mess to catch my attention, but later, many years later, I came to believe God had directed my line of vision. I grabbed at it…and the thought that it was probably just a love letter crossed my mind and I should leave it there, but I needed to go…. I needed to get back home so I just pulled harder and out came a letter and a picture. The picture was of three people, Lucy, Emmerick, and… Miriam. Why this surprised me in a feeling of betrayal I couldn't say, they had already admitted to being friends. I was probably just over-sensitive. I really didn't have time to read the letter, I needed to get back to the house, but I couldn't put off reading the letter any more than a five-year-old could put off opening presents on Christmas morning. What I read in that letter has been forever in my mind. That's the way it is when one finally hears, or in this case, reads the truth.

My mind was numb as I made my way back toward my house. I touched the contents of my pocket, the letter, the picture, the lipstick, and grew angrier and felt more hurt with every step. And on top of everything else, I could be leading someone to my house at this very minute. Someone, possibly the same person who had been in Lucy's apartment could be following me to Miriam right now. But what options did I have? I was nearly distraught thinking about what to do with Miriam…if only I could confide in my father tonight! Maybe there was no other way…maybe it was well past time to get help…real help in dealing with Miriam. I had no way of knowing what had happened to Miriam's parents and there was no way to contact Emmerick. There wasn't anyone else left…I would have to take my father to the barn and tell him. That is if someone wasn't following me. I tried to stick close to the main roads, and offer as little opportunity for someone to hide as they followed me. My fear and paranoia were mounting as I cryptically thought I could be leading death to my door.

CHAPTER NINETEEN

Present Day/ Effie's house

I was sitting on the side of my old bed staring out of the window. I'm not sure how long I had lapsed into silent reflection, but I was brought back to my present by my daughter clearing her throat. I turned to look at the slightly widened eyes of my children. I could tell I had surprised them by telling them more than I ever had before about the war, about some of the things I had experience. I could see they felt the gravity of what I had told them. They had no idea that I had been attacked during the war or that I had been involved in hiding anyone. Jonathon was the first to speak, "Mom, I really had no idea how it was for you during the war. I'm sorry for you, that you experienced such sadness. What a horrible experience!" My sweet and always considerate son. He sat in my old worn wing-backed chair that I have used to hold them and my grandchildren in. Ruth, on the other hand, although always caring, she hid her caring nature behind a veneer of a strong and independent woman who understood very little about weaknesses or mistakes for that matter. "Yes, mother, you certainly did experience some tragedies during the war. You were brutally attacked and that is horrible. Why didn't you tell us before? And, why are you telling us now?"

"Ruth, it was a different time then. More women than anyone will ever know was attacked and raped during the war. Gentile and Jewish women, many German women were abused. It was not something we talked about. Besides, what would be done? Most attackers were soldiers." I tried to defend my decision to keep these things to myself all these years.

"Mother, as bad as that time was for you, you certainly aren't in the same category of Jewish women."

"Ruth! That was totally uncalled for!" defended my Jonathon.

I reached over and laid one hand on each of my children. "No, no... Jonathon...she's quite right. She has no idea how right she is. The Jewish people suffered...at the hands of the Nazi party...but also at our hands too. Even I didn't know of many of the atrocities that so many suffered. I would learn after the war of exactly some of the experiments my... friend...Brigitte had been involved with at Ravensbruck. Some of the women there were placed in pressure chambers and subjected to high altitude tests until they stopped breathing...education for our pilots you see. Some were used in bone grafting experiments while others were used in freezing experiments, also for our pilots, to determine how long they could live if they crashed into freezing water. Others were used in sterilization experiments and others were used for their still youthful skin. Skeletons and skins were collected..."

"Mother!!! Really!! Do you have to be graphic??" Ruth asked as she rose from her position and started folding handkerchiefs lying on my bed.

"Ruth, I am only agreeing with what you said...these poor people did suffer! And so much more than I did! They suffered because we blindly followed a leader bent on exterminating a whole race! They suffered at all of our hands, indeed they suffered at mine!" At this, both of my children, my babies, looked at me with furrowed brows and question marks in their eyes.

"You know, mom, we really don't have to hash all of this out. We understand you experienced and witnessed many horrible things, and now you feel responsible and want to relieve yourself of unnecessary guilt. We both understand that." Jonathon looked pointedly at Ruth.

Ruth sighed and laid down the handkerchief she had folded several times, "Look, I'm sorry; I shouldn't have been so crass. I know you tried to help people mom. Why don't we just let this go, finish packing and go have some dinner?"

I could easily take her advice and just let this all drop. But, selfishly, I have to be relieved of this burden. Even now, someone is going to suffer at my decision. "No, I haven't finished telling you about those days. Please, hear me out." Jonathon looked down at his folded hands that hung between his legs and Ruth sat on the bed next to me. I have kept these secrets for so long, I feel I am about to choke as I try to begin again. Jonathon assured me that nothing I could say would possible effect our relationship or how they loved me. I'm afraid he is wrong.

CHAPTER TWENTY

That Terrible Night

I didn't know what the outcome would be but I had decided on the walk home that I had to tell my father. I could no longer carry the burden of hiding Miriam. It was getting late as I arrived home and our housekeeper had left some stew and bread wrapped in a towel for me. Father wasn't home yet. I was relieved and worried at the same time. I dreaded so badly to tell him, but I had rehearsed my speech on the way home and now that he wasn't here, I was afraid I would lose my nerve. I looked at the stew and felt slightly nauseated. I couldn't eat, but I knew Miriam needed to. I would have to wait until it was completely dark to take food to her. Maybe I should even wait until my father came home. Surely, he would have been here by now if he were able to come today. My nerves were raw, my head was pounding, I was sick at my stomach and I was bone-tired and yet I couldn't be still waiting for dark to come. I was convinced it was just a matter of time before the SS would be forcing their way into my home to arrest me or worse. I couldn't fathom what they would do once they reached the barn…oh!!! Where was my father???? I needed help…I couldn't do this on my own!!! I had to do something…. I looked out of the side of the blackout curtain in the kitchen and realized during my pacing it had grown dark enough to make my way to the barn. My father wouldn't be coming home this late. I decided to go on out to the barn and give Miriam some food. I quickly ran up to my room and found some black sweater and trousers to blend in with the night as much as possible. Now that Miriam had delivered, maybe she could think clearly enough to remember something Emmerick or Lucy might have said to let me know what the next step was supposed to be.

After bagging up her food and water I turned out the light before cracking open the back door. I looked out across our yard toward the little bridge that crossed the creek. I quietly opened the door enough to step out and stood for a few moments letting my eyes acclimate to the darkness. The air was heavy for this time of year. It was as if even the night animals were holding their breath. No crickets, no frogs, no breeze rustling the leaves…just stillness…except something caused me to turn toward the barn. I couldn't tell if it was a human sound or an animal…I couldn't tell if it was a moan or a whimper…was it adult or baby…all I knew was that if I could hear it, so could anyone watching the house. Staying in the shadows as much as possible, I briskly walked toward the barn.

The moon would be numbered among my enemies that night as it glowed brightly on the door of the barn. I used the smaller side door, but this area of the barn was cluttered and the sweat streaming down my face doubled as I tried to feel my way past rakes and hoes and all manner of garden tools; all while carrying Miriam's food. I could hear the half-moan, half-whimper more clearly now and realized it was coming from the loft. She was either sick or hurting or…someone had found her. But, if they had found her…the horrible truth was…I wouldn't be hearing anything from her. I climbed the ladder and peered over the top letting my eyes adjust to the shadows of shapes. I walked the small distance from the ladder to Miriam's cot. As I neared the cot I could see that Miriam was writhing in pain. I sat the food down and knelt next to her.

"Miriam? What is it?? What's wrong? I could hear you in the yard!" I whispered close to her ear. I was so close I could feel the immense heat radiating from her face. I put my hand to her head to confirm she was burning up with fever.

"Effie…I'm…so sorry…. I'm…. bleeding…it feels like fire! I'm burning…from…the inside!! Miriam breathed broken words between gulps of air.

"Ok…. it's ok…I will get help…our housekeeper will be in her room, she can help!"

Miriam grabbed my wrist, "NO! It's too dangerous! It's…too late anyway. Please…just promise me to take care of…." Another pain gripped her and she screamed…I automatically covered her mouth with my hand… "Shhh!!!! Nonsense!! I can get some help for you…she's had children…she will know what to do!!" I leaned closer to her and tried to talk directly in her ear as I smoothed her wet hair off of her forehead. As I leaned back up, I heard it. I heard a sound that gripped me with such fear I was nearly paralyzed…. a car or truck door closed…not loudly, but in a way as not to be heard. My heart accelerated and I tried to strain my ears to hear every sound… I tried to hear where each sound came from. All of my senses were on high alert…ears…eyes…everything performing their function to the highest ability. I heard steps…one person…two…I couldn't tell… Miriam had to be quiet!! I clamped my hand back down on her mouth and looked at her…begging her with my eyes to be quiet. She covered my hand with hers and pushed down even harder over her mouth…. she knew she couldn't keep from crying out in pain and yet to make a sound could mean death for all of us! I was practically laying on top of her willing silence…covering her face…my pulse was bounding…sweat and tears were mingled as they both steadily ran down my face…and the steps were coming ever closer to the barn! The creaking of the barn door raised my panic to new heights and with my free hand I grabbed the blanket and covered Miriam's and my hand over her face… my own breathing seems so loud I buried my head into her chest…and still the footsteps came… I could visualize every step as I heard them…across the floor, around the corner, next to the ladder…my mind screamed that this was it…they had followed me!!! They knew and soon we would all meet Lucy's fate!!! Then the sound of a slow ascension up the ladder…My God my God!!! I was going to die!!! We were all going to die!!! I put all of my weight on Miriam hoping beyond hope if I could keep her quiet and still maybe…. they wouldn't see us…closer and closer…the heavy sound of boots on each rung of the ladder…I was going to scream I just knew it!!! I couldn't take the panic!!! My chest was going to explode…oh God stay away stay away!!! My mind was screaming!!! I didn't even realize how hard I was rocking back and forth…holding Miriam and pushing my head further into her chest!! I was going to be shot!!! The thud of the boot over the ladder finally came and I broke… "NOOOOO NOOOO!!!! Leave us alone!!!! OH GOD PLEASE!!!!!! LEAVE ME ALONE!!!! I DON'T WANT TO DIE!!! PLEASE PLEASE!!! DON'T DO IT DON'T DO IT!!!!! NOOOOO!!!" I screamed and screamed at the top of my lungs!!!

"EFFIE….EFFIE!!!! STOP!!! STOP IT!!!! EFFIE, IT'S ME, STOP!!!"

I was delirious…. I couldn't stop screaming…. they knew my name!!! Large hands were grabbing me by the shoulders and pulled and pulled until my arms were flailing and I was reaching and clawing and trying to make contact to scratch!! Miriam!!! I screamed…. baby squeals and crying erupted as I was pulled up and into a broad chest. "PLEASE NO!!! NO!!!! LET ME GO!!!" I pushed and fought and pushed until I was shaken by my arms, "Effie stop it!! Stop it!! It's me!! It's your father!!! I was pushing against this chest and so overcome with panic he had to say it several more times along with some hard shaking before I realized what he was saying. My legs buckled and I slid down in front of my father as he held me up by my arms. My father dropped to the floor where I was crumpled and drew me into his arms. I heaved and sobbed and gulped for air as my father sat holding me. "Shhh, shhhh…. Effie…. it's ok it's me." He wiped my hair back from my face as it was damp with tears and sweat. "What is all this Effie? Is that a baby??" He moved to stand and I jumped up holding on to his arm. I turned back to Miriam's cot and gathered up the swaddle of whimpering. My father pulled out a lighter and lit it….and saw the horrific site. I stood facing him and attempted to hand him this bundle. I registered the shock in his face as he focused on first me, then the cot behind me. "Father, please, let me explain…this is Miriam…she's Jewish but we had to help her and she was pregnant…and she was making so much noise…I thought they would hear us…she's sick and bleeding…. we have to get some help quickly…oh Father…look…" I juggled the bundle and tried to open the blanket. My father just stood staring behind me…why wasn't he listening to me??…why wouldn't he look at what I was holding…why was he staring behind me….as I turned; I saw the most gruesome site. There, lying on the cot was Miriam…her legs twisted to the side covered in blood…her blankets saturated…her damp, ghostly white face…her black eyes staring straight ahead. "Effie…what happened here?"

I dropped to the floor right next to the cot. I moved in slow motion…I emptied my arms of the now quiet swaddle of blankets…and reached for Miriam. Her mouth was slightly open…my father reached around me and placed his finger to the side of her neck and placed his face in front of her mouth. "Father…she needs…a doctor…" My father turned his face and just looked at me. "No, Effie, she doesn't. I'm afraid she's dead."

"No! No, she can't be…she's just bleeding…I was just talking to her…

no…I was just trying to keep her quiet…no…she must be in shock! Oh God…I did this! I…killed…her!! Father!!! I killed her!!!" I rocked back on my heels and reached back to grab the pants leg of my father. "No, Effie…look…look at all the blood! She must have been hemorrhaging! You couldn't have saved her!" I wouldn't hear it, I knew…I knew the moment I covered her mouth…I didn't want to die…I didn't want whoever was out there to find me. Then she placed her hand on mine and we joined efforts to save the rest of us at her expense.

My father was wise beyond his years and he knew it was past time to take control. Without asking me the particulars of how or why Miriam was here, he began issuing orders to me in order to keep me on track of gathering the blankets, cleaning Miriam, hiding any trace of her being here. Somehow…throughout the night we managed to clean Miriam, put the loft back the way a loft should look, and he dug a grave in our woods. We worked all night to give Miriam the most decent burial we could under the emergent circumstances. The dark night seemed to last longer, just to protect us while we worked. I didn't know what to say at a Jewish burial. All I could say as tears carved a steady path down my bloody, dirty face, was that I was so very sorry. I begged for her forgiveness but it was not to be given…not in this life. We made a make-shift cradle out of a milk crate after we cleaned the loft and quickly packed two suitcases. We would all go to my grandmother's house where Mother was and decide what to do from there.

My eyes would barely stay open as my father drove the long-curved driveway to my grandmother's home. My father felt it was best to get out of Wiesbaden and to the relative safety of her country home. My grandmother had not changed her home or manner of dress since before 1920. That had always been a comfort to me somehow…to know that in this tumultuous world…she was always the same. I hated that I had not been able to see her while she had been sick this year. We all needed to be together as a family right now…and I desperately needed my mother. Before growing so tired during the ride, I had told my father nearly everything that had transpired in my double life since I began my job and met Lucy. When I expected he would look at me in horror, he only placed his hand on mine and squeezed. The depth of his empathy and understanding was not what I expected. I couldn't tell him about the rape. Why, with all the other horrendous things

I'd been involved with I chose to keep this to myself, I didn't know. But… my mother would know. And I needed a mother's advice and teaching now. As I looked into the back seat, into the make-shift crib, I smiled and noted I wasn't the only one who couldn't keep their eyes open.

The sun was breaking through the trees as we pulled up to the house. Once again, the sun appeared to announce the start of a new day, not caring what had happened the night before.

My mother came out of the house; she had not slept after my father phoned her before we left our home. She rushed out to me and held me, she held me so tight I thought she might be trying to absorb all of my guilt and pain into her own being. Why had I been so stupid to not go to my parents sooner, before I was driven to such madness by fear that I committed such a horrible act? That day and night I finally realized the immeasurable depth of love that my family had. Even my grandmother showed such understanding and strength while I told her and my mother the ugly truth. I shared the awful details of my attack and both women held me and cried with me. Over the next several days I cried, slept, changed diapers, and actually listened to advice from my family. A new family needed to be found and my grandmother knew just the place to get help. Her pastor would be able to help. She also nudged at the fact it would do my soul good to have some time to spend talking to the pastor and some time praying.

This part of Germany had miraculously been spared any stray or intentional bombings. So many of the beautiful buildings and churches in other areas had been destroyed, as had so many lives. I walked the relatively short distance to the church. Like most other German towns, the steeple of the church was the center piece of the town. I tugged at the heavy wooden doors and quietly entered the empty sanctuary. My heels sounded magnified as I walked up the middle aisle on ancient rock floors. I walked to a well-worn pew and slid in. Well…here goes…. I'm not sure why I thought what I had to say would be so hard, it's not as if it were a secret from Him. I don't know how long the conversation lasted, but I most definitely remember the next voice I heard.

"Excuse me miss…I'm Dierk…can I help you with anything?"

Chapter Twenty-One

The truth is out

I really had shocked my children. I'm not sure they believed me...they must have thought I had completely lost my mind. They sat in silence, but I could see the wheels turning in Ruth's mind.

"I don't know what to say Mother. Why is this the first time we have ever heard any of this? I don't understand...are you really telling us that you killed that poor woman? And then gave her baby away? Wait a minute...you were raped...the year we were born...are you trying to tell us..." Ruth's voice both trembled with anger and the fear of finding out something she thought she already knew.

"Ruth.... stop.... stop interrogating her!!" Jonathon stood and placed his hand on my shoulder.

"Aren't you listening Jon?? Haven't you heard any of this?? She's trying to tell us that not only are we the product of a horrible act of violence; she killed a woman...AND...gave her baby away!! Why on earth would she tell us this at this time of our lives??" Ruth was now past trembling voice and at full shout. Jonathon shook his head and put both hands on each of my shoulders.

"Babies."

"What? What are you talking about? Why did you just say 'babies'?" Ruth demanded.

"Miriam. She didn't have one baby. She had two...twins. And...I did not conceive from the rape."

The impact of the bomb I had just dropped on my children was unfolding like slow motion war footage. I watched as Ruth grabbed her middle and covered her mouth as she slumped back in the chair...Jonathon left my side and went to his sister, looking back at me as he slid to the floor in front of her. Traitor was written all over his face. So much truth in one word...babies...I could see that all the pieces of this puzzle were still trying to find their rightful place. I just laid out a story that not only was unbelievable, but cold, brutal, life-altering, and selfishly motivated. Why had I waited so long? I couldn't say...maybe I didn't think I would feel the guilt like this during my last years. Somehow when Dierk was still alive, he kept me from feeling guilty. He always kept me reassured that I had actually saved my children's lives. But now, seeing their faces, seeing my reflection in their horrified eyes...I felt the monster that I really was. This could have gone to the grave with me and it wouldn't have mattered...except I felt I needed their forgiveness before I could finally find peace. When I was rehearsing the way, this would go...I didn't anticipate how to handle the shock waves, the fall out that would be left lying around and suffocating the innocent. Should I speak...should I leave them alone...what now? So, yes, even now...just like the terrible night.... self-preservation was foremost in my mind.

"Ruthie...Jon...please...I know this is a horrible thing to find out. But I wanted you to hear it from me...before I was no longer able to tell you." A most pathetic attempt to begin the explanations.

"Mother! Just stop...I can't believe this...I can't believe what you are saying! I can't even look at you right now!! What on earth could you gain by telling us this...this.... disgusting story! I have to get out of here! I don't want to hear anymore of this!! How could you unload all of this on us?! Do you have any idea of what you have just done? I've always known you to be harsh and selfish and spoiled...but this.... you are unbelievable!"

"Ruth...let's just calm down! We just need to calm down...let's not start saying things we will regret! Let's just go outside...walk around. Mother...we just need...I don't know...we just need to be away from you right now. Please, don't say anymore! We can't think clearly!" Jonathon pulled Ruth to her feet and protectively wrapped his arm around her shoulder and led her out of my room and down the stairs. As I heard the door open and close I looked out the window and watched my poor shocked children walk across the yard. I watched as Ruth's shoulders finally slumped and she leaned into her brother's chest. They stood next to the picnic table and tree swing that they had grown up playing on. I leaned my forehead on the window pane and traced my babies with my finger. No, I didn't carry them, but I did deliver them...and if Dierk was right, I did save their lives. But more than that, I love them. I loved them from the night they were delivered until this very moment. I didn't know if I would have the opportunity to tell them...how much they meant to me and to their father. I thought back to the first time I heard his voice, 'Excuse me miss...I'm Dierk...can I help you with anything?' I wish he were here to ask me that now.

CHAPTER TWENTY-TWO

Dierk

I had been crying and praying the first time we met. My eyes were red and swollen, underlined by dark half-moons, my nose was running and I didn't have the first bit of make-up on. But over the years, he said so many times that I was the prettiest girl he had ever seen. I had gone to the church to speak to the pastor about finding a family for the twins, but I was so torn. Just in the short time I had been surrogate mother to them I had come to love them, but my family felt sure this would be the right thing to do. I had expected to see the aging pastor when I heard the voice, but when I looked up, I saw a young, brown-haired, blue-eyed man standing over me with the most authentic look of caring I believe I had ever seen. He had the look of someone who made you feel like telling them everything about yourself in one setting. I felt an immediate connection, different from anything I had felt with Emmerick. This felt like a safe place or a warm Sunday afternoon rest in the sun. I began by telling him who I was and who my grandmother was. He, of course, knew of my grandmother and spoke very complimentary of her. I just wanted to blurt the whole truth out and say, "Now fix it!" but I did explain myself a little slower than that.

"I'm at a loss as to how to ask for the help that I need without scaring you away." I opened up apologetically.

"Please, this is why I am here...why the church is here. I don't scare easily and if I can help, please let me." Dierk spoke with a deep timbre and authoritative voice filled with genuine concern.

I didn't begin with the how and the why I ended up harboring a young Jewish girl, I at least spared him that at first, but I did tell him that I had a young friend who had passed away and now I was caring for her twins.

I did tell him that she was Jewish which let him know immediately of the heaviness of the situation. I admitted something to him that I think I had just come to realize myself. I told him my original hope was to come to the church to find someone to take the children, but even as I was saying it my heart grew so heavy I thought it might break. It was impossible for me to keep them as a single person so what options were there? Dierk sat quietly for a few moments contemplating the right advice.

"How long will you be here with your grandmother? I would need some time to think about the right thing to do."

"I'm not sure...as long as I need to be I suppose." I knew that finding a family was the best thing, but I already felt like they were mine.

"I tell you what, let me think about this and I will come check on you and the children if you don't mind."

"Just knowing that I'm being helped is a great relief Mr. ....."

"Dierk, please. I'm not sure of your age nor would I ask, but I don't think I'm quite old enough to be a mister to you yet." He grinned with those crystal-clear eyes and warm smile. It felt like weights were being lifted. Not only had I confessed to my parents and now had their help and support, but I had spent a few minutes trying to mend my relationship to God, and now another trust-worthy person would be able to help. I felt lighter than I had in months. Dierk walked me to the door and when he opened the door to reveal the bright early sunshine, I found myself smiling instead of cursing the sun for mocking my despair.

True to his word, Dierk came to my grandmother's house nearly every day for the next couple of weeks. He was being very cautious about asking around about available families who could afford to take the twins. We were adamant about not separating them. He was sorry to say he had not had any luck so far. He also knew the longer I had them, the harder it would be to let them go. Over the course of his visits we often took walks and eventually I told him most of the history of my life up to this point. It would take years for me to confide everything to him, but he was so patient and was an amazing listener those first few weeks we became quick and close friends. He spent time holding the babies and I even caught him cooing more than once. My mother and grandmother were like new mothers themselves as they held and fed and changed the babies. I was being lulled into some kind of suspended fairy tale, it was as if the war could not reach this far in the country and I began to fantasize that this was my new life and my new family. I also started noticing little things about Dierk that I'm sure a girl usually wouldn't notice about a clergy member. It amused me in later years how fickle a young girl's heart can be. Just a few months before, I didn't think there could be anyone for me except for Emmerick. If I had any doubts that he wasn't my Mr. Right, the letter I found at Lucy's apartment laid all doubts to rest. He was not mine and never had been.

My father had to go back to work but would come out to Grandmothers every weekend and sometimes once or twice through the week. There weren't many questions asked concerning our whereabouts, my father's simple explanation of my grandmother needing me and my mother were sufficient. It was during one of his mid-week trips that my fairy-tale little world took another turn. Father came home one evening just as we were about to sit down to dinner. As had become his habit, Dierk was eating with us. As we were finishing dinner, my father stated he had something for me.

"Oh, Effie, I almost forgot. A letter came in the post for you this week. I believe it's from one of your friends." He reached in his coat pocket and handed me the letter. At first, I was confused because my first thoughts were of my most recent relationships. As I looked at the envelope, I realized it was from Brigitte. This was not all together odd, but it had been a while since I had heard from her or Anne. So much had happened; I had almost forgotten my girl-hood friends. I pocketed the envelope and decided to not interrupt the evening with Dierk and my father to read it right away. We ate and had vacillating conversations between the most recent war news, how the babies were doing, had there been any luck finding a new family, recalling how much better my grandmother was feeling especially while she was caring for the twins and what was happening in Wiesbaden. After dinner, Dierk had asked to speak to my father so my mother and grandmother and I took the twins outside to sit and enjoy twilight. My grandmother was holding Ruth and my mother was holding Jonathon. I sat watching my two mentors while breathing in the cooling evening air. How was it that this little piece of Germany felt so far removed from the devastation happening everywhere else? It was the surroundings; it was the love of the people around me that made the difference. Just then I remembered the letter in my pocket. I felt uneasiness, I should be more excited to hear from an old friend...but all that had transpired had proven that she was not the friend or the person I once thought, and neither was I. I felt more of a dread to read the letter than anything. Once again, I pushed that task aside until the evening was over and Dierk was gone and everyone else was in bed.

That time came sooner than I would have liked. It was becoming more difficult to say goodbye to Dierk and hoping to get to see him the next day but not wanting to ask to. Everyone was asleep; Ruth and Jonathon were sleeping next to each other in their make-shift crib. I touched their warm soft heads and watched their little eyelids twitch and their tongues move back and forth as if they were dreaming of nursing. They had such sweet little faces, so soft and smooth with their black eyelashes fluttered across the top of their cheeks. Miriam would be so proud of her babies and as much as I was coming to love them, I felt sure her heart would have burst with love for two such amazing little people. My heart ached for the loss of their mother and for the way Miriam's short life ended. I still carried the guilt of responsibility for her even though my family had assured me many times that her death could not have been avoided. But they weren't in my heart. They didn't know the jealousy that I harbored and the knowledge that there was a possibility that jealousy kept me from doing everything I could for her.

I smoothed their blankets over their tiny little backs and let my hands rest there while I felt their bodies expand with their breaths. I felt that I could stand there and watch them all night. But their night was not nearly long enough for rest as they would be hungry again in just a few hours so I left their sides and sat on my bed. I finally took the letter from Brigitte out of my pocket and opened it. Sighing deeply, I flipped through the couple of pages and shuffled them back together to begin reading.

"Dearest Effie,

I hope this letter finds you well. I am of course still at work for our fuehrer at Ravensbruck doing what I can for the mother land. I don't need to remind you, of all people, how important it is to stay the course. I recently heard from Anne. It appears that she is quite enjoying her new role as a wife. My suspicion is that she will be filling another role of motherhood before much longer. As for me, I prefer as I always have to stay focused on my calling and work. Besides, the only person I would consider as a closer companion than a friend is not stationed here anymore so I no longer see him as often as I did before. I would love to share more of the fascinating discoveries that have been made by our doctors here, but I fear that I must be discriminate as one never knows who will read our correspondence. This brings me to the point of my letter. I would like to see you the next time I am home. I long to visit with you and hear about all you have been in to. You see, I know that you have been quite the busy bee. I have heard how hard you have been working at the base, just like all faithful Germans, doing their part. I have heard that you have made several new friends, which is always an asset in times like these. I hope that you know them well, dear friend. One can never be too sure these days. Knowing how dedicated you are to our country and our vision, I know that you would never knowingly entertain undesirables. But, you have always been so kind and welcoming…remember the little animals you used to try to rescue when we were children? I believe you would try to save a common gutter rat, if it played on your emotions. I must go for now dearest friend, but I will be to see you soon. In fact, it will be a great opportunity to see the one person I would consider a relationship with. I don't mean to be mysterious; of course, you and Anne must know the only guy from our group I would count as equal! Sepp is now working out of Frankfurt…so close to home that I hope we can all three get together very soon and have a nice long visit! Until then, my friend, keep working for the Reich as we all are. I look forward to seeing a childhood friend that I have recently come to understand so much better!

Faithful,
Brigitte"

CHAPTER TWENTY-THREE

Present Day

"Hey Ruthie, I'm glad you called. I've been worried about you. I'm glad we could meet up for dinner." Jonathon rounded the corner of the fairly secluded booth at one of Ruth's favorite restaurants. Ruth slid over as her brother motioned to the waiter. After asking for water with lemon and salmon salad, Jonathon took his glasses off and absently used his napkin to wipe them off.

"So, have you seen her? Since we dropped her off?" Ruth asked as she twisted the straw paper until tiny paper balls fell onto the table cloth.

"No, no I haven't been to see her. I want to, but I just haven't been able to yet. I'm assuming you haven't either. We need to talk about all this Ruth, we need to wrap our minds around it...move past it."

"Well, Jon, I just don't think I can 'move past it'. The lies our entire lives have been based on...we don't even know who are real mother is! For heaven's sake Jonathon...we are Jewish and didn't even know it! I mean, who is our father?? We couldn't even get to that little truth with all the shocking revelations! And why now?? I just don't get it...why now.... we are getting old ourselves! We have lived our whole lives without knowing and all of a sudden she decides to unburden herself?" Ruth's voice steadily grew louder.

Jonathon laid his hand on hers in an attempt to quiet her. "Sis, I understand...I don't have any answers...but I do know that working through this is for the best. She wouldn't have told us if she didn't have a good reason. We don't know what really happened back then. I just have to try to understand that times were different. I think we should try to talk to her again."

"You've got to be kidding! I can't even think about going close to her let alone listen to more of her confessions! No, I just can't. Not now.…... maybe not ever!" Ruth declared with absolute resolution.

"Ruth, don't say that. I know you are hurt, I am too, but she raised us, she took care of us…we are still the same family. And I for one want answers, don't you? Hasn't anything she said piqued your curiosity at all?" Jonathon spoke in hushed tones as the waiter brought the salad and Ruth's pasta.

Ruth half-heartedly smiled at the waiter and paused until he left. She sighed and took her fork and twirled a small piece of spaghetti around it, yet didn't lift it to her mouth. "Jon, I just feel so…... lost or betrayed or something…I can't even articulate what I'm feeling! Who are we? Who was our mother? And here's another unfathomable question…we were raised as Christians, yet we are Jewish…. how does that work? I mean, I have Jewish friends…but do you even know how we are supposed to incorporate all of this? Good grief Jon my head is literally spinning!"

Jonathon laid his fork aside and leaned against the back of the booth. "No, Ruth, I really don't. But I do know that we are who we are. Think about it Ruth, are we going to change our lives over this? We have our own families, our own children, careers…none of that changes, we just have to figure out how to embrace this information…. or not. You know, we don't have to do anything. We can just carry on like we always have. Or, we can dig deeper and find that we may have a pretty rich heritage that we may want to pass on to our children and grandkids. I think it's a state of mind Ruthie. Maybe we need to consider…forgiving her….and learn what we can while she's still with us."

Ruth stared at her plate. Hot tears of confusion and hurt…and a little mixture of shame over the way she had spoken to her…mother…. pooled in her eyes. She formed a ghost of a smile and patted Jonathon's hand. She couldn't fathom forgiveness at this point…but it always was hard to debate Jon's optimism. "I hear what you're saying, Jon. It's always been easier for you to bounce back after a fight with her. There's something blocking that with me and her and now this…. I just don't know how to deal with this. I don't know how to begin to forgive her. How is it so easy for you?"

"It's not easy, Ruth. I'm confused, I'm angry, I don't know what to do with what she told us. But, I do know that she raised us, I do know that I love her and her love for us has always been real. Now that we know how we came to be her children… well, that speaks volumes of how much she must have always loved us. She saved us Ruth. I don't understand the life-long secret, but the only way to get a better understanding is to swallow our pain and confusion, forgive her, and let her help us understand. And by the way, the reason you struggle with her and always have is because you are just like her. Biological daughter or not, you are like her." Jon sat back in the booth, and let Ruth take in what he had said. He didn't know he felt all of those emotions until they just came out.

After several minutes of napkin twisting, Ruth finally spoke barely above a whisper. "Well, you certainly put me in my place. I get it. I'm sure you're right… not about our similarities… but if nothing else I suppose we need to at least see her. See where that takes us."

CHAPTER TWENTY-FOUR

The me of just a few months before would have tucked the letter away and devised a scheme to handle it myself, but if I had learned anything, I had learned to ask for help when I needed it and I needed it now. I didn't even wait until the morning. As soon as I finished reading Brigitte's letter, I went to my parent's room and shared the letter with my father. He knew the intent of the letter and the implied danger. He shared it with my mother and she too knew something would need to be done and done quickly. The solution wouldn't be formulated that night, but I knew as I went back to my room that I had done the right thing to involve my parents. There could only be one implication of her letter…she knew about Lucy and Emmerick and what we had done these past few years. Brigitte had so many cruel contacts, I naturally thought she would be turning us over any day now if she had not already. I had no idea what had happened to Emmerick that last night, and I still had a sliver of hope that Lucy was somewhere…. maybe hiding and recovering…maybe she took the plan to get Miriam to Munich and turned it into her own. The one thing I did know, I could not try to find out…contact them…anything until… well I'm not sure there would be an 'until'. I still thought of them every day, many times a day, and wondered and hoped they were ok. They had to be worried sick about Miriam and part of me was glad I had been able to avoid telling them what happened to her. Right then I needed to concentrate on finding the twins the best home, and try to finish healing from all that had happened. Time with my family…and with Dierk…was like a soothing balm on all the exposed wounds I had. My family was the very definition of supportive, and Dierk, well he was so unbelievably kind and funny! His ability to make me laugh during those days was nothing short of miraculous! And he did it often! It was as if he had taken me and the twins on as his personal mission to minister to and I gladly accepted.

"Effie, I believe I found parents for the twins." We had just finished one of our regular weekly dinners and were sitting outside on my grandmother's swing that faced her tiny, tidy little rose garden. My feet stopped the swing and I looked straight ahead. I knew this was what he was supposed to do, I knew that this was for the best, but as he said it my heart fell to the bottom of my stomach. It had to have actually left my chest and landed squarely in my stomach because the pain in my chest could only be from my heart being torn out and the pain in my stomach had to be from a hard hit. "I see", was all I could get out.

Dierk laid his hand on my shoulder, "I think I have found the best people to love the twins and raise them as their very own. I know she will love and protect them with her life...because she already has."

His words weren't making sense... "I don't understand..."

"I know we have only known each other a very short time, but I can say that I have come to care about you and about what happens to the babies. I think we should...get married....and raise them."

I couldn't answer, I still wasn't completely comprehending...he couldn't possibly want to give up his position here to marry someone who was already used and raise children he had no part in creating.

"You don't have to answer right now, maybe you want to think about it until...."

"No."

"No, you won't marry me?"

"No, I don't need to think about it."

"Are you saying yes or no? I'm sorry Effie I'm not following you."

"I'm saying yes. But I'm not sure you know what you are asking for." I looked down at my folded hands...how would I explain to him that he wouldn't be my first...I couldn't marry him unless he knew the truth... could I?

"I know what I'm asking and why I'm asking it. We can move to Zurich, I have family there, and when this war is over, if you want to come back we can. If you don't then we will make a home somewhere else. I have talked to your father about this...he approves. So, if you're really saying yes then I'd say we should tell your family and move forward with the ceremony as soon as possible."

The first thought that came to me was that I would keep the babies… they belonged with me…I had never been more certain of that. My second thought was that I doubted I would ever meet a kinder man. "I'm really saying yes."

So, that's how it came to be. That's how it came to be that I would become Mrs. Dierk Kohl. The proposal was a mixture of a heart-felt sentiment coupled with an attempt to get away from Brigitte or any threat she could pose…and the life of the twins. The next few days were a whirlwind of father speaking to Dierk, Dierk speaking to the senior pastor, and Dierk contacting family in Zurich. Marriages were arranged for far less important reasons than saving the lives of two babies and I already felt a great fondness and respect for Dierk. He professed a great fondness for me and felt it was the hand of God intervening in our lives.

The night before our hastily planned wedding was one of the most nerve wracking nights of my life. I had nearly talked myself out of marrying Dierk simply so that I wouldn't have to tell him what had happened to me. I was a bundle of nerves, nothing he could say was right, I was snappy with everyone around me. I was in such a torment…. I had to do this to keep the twins…and I did care about him…so much so I didn't want him to have to try and mend one more area of my being. Dierk left right after dinner after a small peck on my cheek and a whispered promise that it was just last-minute jitters and everything would be fine. I turned into my room early and paced and sat and paced some more. Finally, my mother came in with hot tea and sat on the bed without saying a word.

Her presence alone was enough to break the veneer I had covering me the last couple of days. I sat on the floor at her feet and laid my head on her knees. She petted my head and my cheeks until silent tears started to trail down my face.

"Effie, you can't keep carrying this…this guilt. You didn't do anything wrong. That man that attacked you was not a man at all but an animal. He was a cruel thief and he has taken enough from you, don't let him rob you of the joy that is so close to being yours." My mother knew what was wrong with me all along.

"Mother, I feel so dirty and ashamed!! I've already been touched in such a hateful way…how am I supposed to let Dierk touch me the way he expects to as my husband?"

"Effie, I can't imagine the depth of pain you feel and it breaks my heart that I wasn't at home for you that night. It wakes me up at night to think of what was happening to my one baby out there alone…it's a horrible crime and if I could get my hands on him…. I don't know what I would do, but I imagine I would fight him with everything in me. But I refuse to let him steal the rest of your life! You need to just talk to Dierk…be honest from the beginning. You can't hide that kind of thing from someone you will be spending your life with. He seems very compassionate, and it might be hard, but with honesty and patience, you two can grow into a loving and fulfilling relationship." She continued to stroke my head and wiped my tears with her monogrammed handkerchief. "Oh, my sweet baby…. what I wouldn't give to have been there for you. But let me be here now and help you heal from this."

I wrapped my arms around my mother's legs and loved her all the more for her understanding and wisdom. As luck, would have it, the wedding the next morning and the subsequent hasty move to Zurich allowed me several more days before Dierk approached me about staying in the same room and sleeping in the same bed. Over the years, I had often thought I fell in love with him the day he introduced himself at the church, but the truth of it is, I believe it had to be the night he asked if I was ready to sleep together. He obviously sensed my hesitation and nervousness, but not for the reasons he thought. I told him that night. I told him everything that had transpired since the day I met Lucy and Emmerick. I told him every detail of the attack. He could have been disgusted and could have annulled our marriage, but he did neither. He poured more love and kindness into me than I thought was possible, and my mother had been right. Over the course of our first few weeks of married life, Dierk taught me that the once vile act that had been enacted on me was nothing like what it was to be loved in that way. He was the very definition of gentleness and kindness and patience. And with those qualities he guided us into a marriage I had given up on having.

So, we married, moved to Zurich and later to America, raised our babies and did not look back. At least not for a while.

CHAPTER TWENTY-FIVE

World War II officially ended September 2, 1945. The Allies accepted surrender from Germany on May 8, 1945 so from our perspective that was the end. I was 24 years old, married and had two growing children. We had lived in Zurich until we were able to secure passage to America without causing raised eyebrows. Dierk found us a sweet little farm to live on, he found work in the local town in insurance sales and estate auctions. I suppose that was where our love of antiques began. He would sneak me and the kids into the auction houses to view the items before the next days' auction. We always had the most fun looking at everything and wishing we had this piece or that. I was like so many other stay at home mothers, I took care of our home, our kids, and Dierk. Life took on a serenity that was often thought of as boring by the kids, but was such a relief for us. I could go two or three days sometimes without dwelling on the war or the parts we played in it. But then I would hear a song or run into someone at the drug store who reminded me of Lucy or one of the "group" and my mind would dredge up all the fears and regrets again. I would talk to Dierk about it, but even I got tired of trying to make myself feel better, much less keep expecting him to fill that role. I don't remember the exact trigger, but one day in the spring of 1950 my mind was forced back into thinking about the old gang, what had happened to them, did they know about me…did they care? I always had that little pesky tug at the back of my mind that someone out there knew that I had helped Jews escape and what I had done to Miriam. I don't know what made this bout of melancholy any different than the others, but this time I got angry and decided enough was enough. I was suddenly determined to face those ghosts and get rid of them once and for all.

The trip back to Germany was a far cry from the trip to America. We had sailed to America, now I was taking an airplane back. In 1950, people treated air travel as quite an extravagant event. Ladies still dressed in skirts and heels while men had on suites. Nothing like the flannel pajama pants and t-shirts that people fly in today. And unlike the first trip, this time I made the trip alone while Dierk and the children stayed home. The children of course knew they were German, but they knew nothing of how we all became a family. This trip was intended to close some doors. My grandmother had been gone since the year we left. My parents had stayed on at her house in the country after the war. There was much less destruction in the country and fewer reminders of that unimaginable time. We wrote as often as we could and I sent countless pictures of the grandchildren they helped save. Although I tried not to ask about my once dear "friends", I couldn't help but hint in my letters that I was still afraid of one of them finding me and at the very least exposing the truth to my children. Even though the war was long over, the memories for those of us who lived through it were not. I didn't think of them every day, but often. And though the nightmares were less occurring they were as detailed and real as ever. Miriam's eyes were never far from my mind. Not only because I dreamed about that terrible night of her death, but because I looked at them every time I looked at my daughter. I loved my children with a fierceness that I'm sure suffocated them most of their lives but it was driven from the fear that Brigitte knew or Sepp would reappear or their father. I kept telling myself that if he did make it through the war I would somehow feel it. I would somehow know he was still there.

From my subtle inquiries, my mother wrote that she had seen Anne and her children the last time she was in Wiesbaden. She said she was just as pleasant as she was when we were teenagers and her children seemed happy and healthy. Mother was passing along the well wishes from Anne who mother had skillfully avoided telling my whereabouts. Anne insisted that my mother ask me to visit her the next time she saw me. After reading and re-reading the letter multiple times, I decided I was tired of not knowing. I was tired of looking over one shoulder waiting for one of them to show up. Dierk was not excited at all about the idea of me returning to Germany; however, he knew I missed my parents and a visit with them would do me some good. He pleaded with me right up until I boarded the plane to not see Anne while I was there or try to find any others. The war wasn't over for everyone in Germany. I never lied to Dierk, so I just smiled and patted his chest as we hugged.

His prediction had been right. My visit to see my parents was just what I needed. I didn't realize how much I really did miss them until we were sitting in the comfy living room of the country house laughing and looking at pictures and just being together. The room truly had not changed since the day I got married and left for Zurich. Oh, mother had brought several of her own things from our house but it was all still reflective of my grandmother. By the night of my first day there, the elephant in the room could no longer be danced around. My mom was in my room telling me goodnight when I asked her where to find Anne. She was hesitant to tell me, but in the end, she did tell me that she was in our old neighborhood. She gave her opinion that a visit wasn't necessary, to let it go. I had to do it. I was driven to face whatever was always looming behind me, over my shoulder just hovering and waiting to destroy the life Dierk and I had created. Visiting Anne seemed like the easiest and safest way to start looking back. Mother would only go along with it is she and my father drove me and stayed close by. I whole-heartedly agree; I wanted answers, but I certainly wasn't going to do this on my own.

It wasn't difficult to spot her as I walked from the café where my parents were going to wait for me. The cobblestone roads were once again bustling with people going to work, shopping, eating and getting back to living. I passed through the square and looked up at the old clock tower. I could smell the yeast of breads rising coming from the open windows of the bakery on the corner. I could still feel the nervous anticipation I felt as I walked these streets the night I met Lucy. Then I thought of the night I met Emmerick at her apartment. Then all the thoughts rushed back like a movie fast forwarding. I shook my head in an effort to shake my thoughts. I walked toward the slender beauty that she still was as she was sweeping her front sidewalk and directing a small army of little people. My heels must have alerted her to my approach, but as she looked my way, a slow dawning of recognition came over her face. We didn't rush to each other and hug like long lost friends. I approached the gate of her white fence and she approached with the broom held in front of her like a shield.

"Oh...my...Effie?? Is that really you?"

"Yes, it's really me." I repeated the obvious to give us both a second to react appropriately. "I'm visiting my parents. Mother said she ran into you not long ago. I thought it would be nice to see you while I'm here." I tried not to lie but there it was.

"Um, well, of course! Please, come up and have a seat. You will have to excuse me, I need to round up my bunch and take them in to their grandmother. Armin's mother lives with us."

Anne came back out smoothing her hair and apron. "So, wow...it's been nearly nine years. How have you been?"

"During the war I went to Zurich. After you got married and Brigitte went to Ravensbruck, my grandmother became ill. My mother ended up staying with her and my parents didn't feel it was safe here." Not *really* a lie.

"I just can't believe you are here! You must stay and see Armin when he comes home tonight! What a surprise it will be!" Anne replied with her own half-truth.

"Thank you, but no. I'm here with Mother and Father and they are waiting for me at the café. I just wanted to see you while I was here, catch up a little. You have lovely children! The last time I received a letter from Brigitte during the war, she thought you might be ready for the role of mother. Looks like it suites you well." Maybe the mention of Brigitte would elicit a response. I watched her face closely, but only saw a split second of her eyes turning downward.

Anne laughed, "Well, she was right! Armin and I were expecting very soon after our wedding. Gosh that seems so long ago, doesn't it?"

My mind flashed to the night of her mother's funeral and the walk home with Sepp and his disgusting advances. No, it didn't seem that long ago. "Well, time does go by quickly like our parents always said when we were younger. So, how is Armin?"

"As handsome as ever! He is working in Frankfurt. Suit and tie man now. He will be sorry he missed you. He won't be happy that I couldn't talk you into staying."

"Please tell him you tried but I could not be persuaded. I really can't keep my parents waiting. My father will have already eaten too many pastries as it is. I was thinking about trying to see some other friends while I'm here though, even for just a quick visit. How are the rest of our friends? I should look Brigitte up while I'm here." I watched carefully for any sign that she knew about Brigitte's subtly threatening letter all those years ago.

With a smile, Anne reached over and squeezed my hand, "Let me take you to her. I was planning on a visit soon myself. It's not far, just a short walk from here. It won't take long and then I will walk you back to the café and say hello to your parents."

I should have known they would all end up back in our neighborhood. Nice and cozy and happy in our childhood home just like nothing had ever happened while I lived half a world away hiding out like a fugitive. With my stomach slowly tying itself into little knots I smiled widely and said, "That would be nice. Then I really do need to go. I'm actually married myself and I have two children who will be waiting to hear from me tonight."

"That's wonderful Effie! I don't get to Zurich much, but I will have to make a special effort now. Let me tell Armin's mother, I will be right back."

I couldn't believe I was about to come face to face with the very person I was sure knew about me, Miriam, Emmerick, and Lucy and all the rest of the Jewish people we helped. I tried to draw on the fact that I was older, had been through a war and devastating events, and there was nothing I should fear from her. Anne came back out minus the apron and we walked out of her gate and took a left, opposite direction of the café. We continued on with small talk as we walked. We rounded a corner just right outside of the town area and started walking down a country road. I wasn't aware there were many houses out this direction, but obviously more had changed during my exile than I realized.

"Well, here we are. Just up this hill." Anne looked toward the little country church and attached parsons house. My first thought was that Brigitte had married a clergyman and found God. We rounded the small white wooden church that had escaped any scarring from the war.

"Here we are." Anne motioned her hand to the area next to the parsonage. I looked to her and back again. We walked forward and came to stop in front of a fairly new granite headstone. "She's right here."

I couldn't make words come out of my open mouth. I slowly reached out and touched the top of the stone. The last date read 'October 5, 1945.'

Anne stood for several minutes before she began to unravel the explanation. "Effie, after the war...many of the SS were executed, including women guards for their parts in the camps. I went to her trial There were several women guards on trial that day. They said that horrific experiments were done at Ravensbruck and that she helped the doctors there conduct them. I had no idea. I suppose I was so wrapped up in being married and having a new baby…I just buried my head in the sand and acted as if none of it was real. The American soldiers made a lot of Germans walk through the camps while there were still bodies decaying there. I wasn't one of them, but I was just as guilty. I didn't physically hurt anyone, but I didn't look beyond my own door to see what was being done to so many innocent people. Armin was able to essentially disappear for a while. He wasn't important enough to track down I suppose. We eventually made it back here. He has so many regrets Effie. You have no idea at the nightmares he has. He became a changed man you know. I think we were all blinded to an extent…all of us…except a few." Anne looked at me with an expression that told me she knew more about me than I realized. "You don't have to say anything Effie. Brigitte wrote to me more than once ranting and raving about you and your 'new friends'. She was convinced you were harboring Jews, but I don't think she ever had proof. I think the bottom line was that she was very jealous of you. She knew that Sepp liked you before the war even started. We always teased her, but she really did like him, a lot. They eventually ended up together, she wanted to get married but I think the chances of that happening after he had already slept with her were very slim. I think she came to realize that as well and the only direction she could spew her venomous jealousy was toward you. She was convinced you were what was standing between them. She threatened to tell Sepp you were hiding Jews so many times, I think she actually fabricated a story he believed. The last I spoke with her before the end of the war, I told her how absolutely ridiculous she was being, that you were in no way interested in Sepp and she needed to stop creating these lies. Before she could ever put a plan into action, the war turned swiftly and she was arrested along with the others. They also executed Sepp. So, you see Effie, there's no reason to stay away. I wanted to reach out to you so many times, but I thought I should just let it go and let you have your life. Nothing ever came of her obsession and I wasn't even sure you knew any of it. I'm sorry if I was wrong."

I was in complete disbelief. I couldn't believe they were gone….and had been gone for quite some time. All this time I could have felt freedom. I felt joy and resentment. I could have hugged Anne or slapped her…either would have matched my emotions. Anne hesitantly put her arm around my shoulders, "Effie, I'm so sorry…I underestimated how hard it would hit you to know all of this. Come on let's get you out of here. I'm going to walk you back to your parents."

Anne attempted a few times to start the conversation back on our walk, but I just could not wrap my mind around it. We reached the café and they exchanged pleasantries with Anne. She reached out to hug me, which I allowed and we got in the car and left. My parents had to have been full of questions, but wisely let me digest before talking about it. Once I did tell them, they were as surprised as I was, but didn't carry the same shock. They were glad that I wouldn't have to feel like there was someone behind me waiting for just the right time to make a move and uproot my and Dierk's life. Those weren't the only people who could have an impact on our family. There were still two people who could come back into my life. That was to be the second part of my plan in returning to Germany. There had to be some way to find out about Emmerick and Lucy.

I only had two more days with my parents before I had to get back on a plane to head home, so I questioned myself why I was spending part of that time trying to find anyone who worked with me and Lucy or who knew where they were. But, much like when I was younger, I took off in my own direction and told them I would be spending the day in Wiesbaden, shopping…taking photos…buying gifts for the kids…and I did, but I also planned on some foot work to track down anyone who knew anything and who was willing to talk about it. I had compiled a very short list of places that I thought I might run into people we all three knew. The first place was the bistro where I saw Emmerick and Lucy for the first time. The image facing me as I approached the café was nowhere near as haunting as it was when I thought back on those secret nights out. Time and daylight had a way of clearing out any lingering shadows or ghosts. I knew I was grasping at straws to try this…but I felt I had to at least try. I sat in the bistro for quite a while then took my tea to a table outside. Up to that point I had not seen anyone familiar. I took in the scenery that really had not changed that much or suffered much damage. There were still times I missed Germany. I sat long enough to decide it wasn't accomplishing anything except a good bout of melancholy and it was getting late in the day. Then, just as I was about to leave money on the table and move on, my eye was caught be a girl that we used to work with. I couldn't remember her name, but she ate lunch with Lucy at times and she would be at Lucy's apartment get-togethers every so often. She was coming out of a dress shop across the street so I quickly tossed the bill down on the table, grabbed my purse and gloves and tried to follow quickly behind. Before I could catch up she ducked into a butcher's shop. I continued clicking my heels across the part cobblestone part cement sidewalk until I reached the shop. I didn't have a plan that included the part where I actually found someone who might know something. So, I stood like a creepy stalker outside of the butcher shop looking at the weeks' specials written boldly on the window. With the ding of the little bell on the door, she was out again and heading across the street. Once again, I followed, obviously thinking I was stealth in my movements behind her. She went into the hat shop and I followed. I studiously looked at all the new styles of hats and thought how each would look on Ruthie. I stayed right around the perimeter of where this girl was, hoping to blend in with the rest of the shoppers. I wanted to make sure it was the same one we worked with all those years ago. Once I had determined that she was, I would approach her and what??

"What??!! Why are you following me?" I was snapped back into reality with her sudden turn and rapid fire of questions.

"I... I'm sorry, you may not remember me but we used to work together...during the war. I'm Effie." I tried the simple and direct method.

"Oh...yeah...you do look familiar. So why are you following me?"

She wasn't swayed into a false reunion with fake smiles.

"I've been gone for a long time...I'm back visiting family and wanted to see some old friends but I'm having a hard time finding some of them."

"Maybe your friends don't want to be found. Maybe they can't be... there was a war you know." Wow, even if we weren't acquaintances or friends...she was definitely abrupt.

"Look, I'm sorry, I should've just walked right up to you. I just wanted to make sure you were who I thought you were. Can I buy you a tea or coffee and maybe you can help me unravel some of the whereabouts of my friends?" I put the hat back on the stand as the clerk raised her eyebrow at us as to question if we were buying or not. The girl looked at her watch and said, "I don't have a lot of time. I have to pick up my children. Just ask me what you want to ask." She too placed a hat back on the hat stand and started making her way by me to the door.

"Do you know where Lucy is?"

She stopped short of opening the door, and for just a split-second I thought I touched a nerve.

"No." She reached for the door and was gone again.

"No? That's it?" I followed her out onto the sidewalk where she pulled out her cigarettes and lit one.

"Terrible habit I hear, but what do they know? Look, I haven't seen Lucy since the war. I'm sorry. I don't have anything to tell you. Now, who else are you looking for or was it just her?" She blew smoke in the opposite direction of me and stood with her arms crossed ready to tell me no about somebody else.

"Do you remember Emmerick?"

"Of course...he was gorgeous. All the girls at the office flirted with him or at least tried. He was pretty set on one person it seemed." She tapped her cigarette out on her metal cigarette case and place the unsmoked butt back in it.

"Have you seen him?"

With an exasperated sigh, she replied, "No. No I haven't seen him since we worked together. He stopped working at that office right after the last round up. I don't know where he went after that. Look, Effie, is it? Why don't you just see who you can and move on? Why drudge up all those people? Maybe they didn't even make it and if they did, they probably would have found you if they wanted to. I have to go. Did you need anything else?" She tugged her kid glove back into place and turned away from me.

"No, I suppose not. I hate to ask, but I can't remember your name."

She started across the street with a half wave. "goodbye Effie."

No name, no smile, no information. Except the fact that she was way too testy and evasive. But one thing she said was true. I needed to see who I could see before going back home. I popped back into the hat shop, bought Ruthie two hats and ventured on to other shops to get something for Jon. Then I headed straight back to the country and to my parents to spend my last day and half in Germany with the people that really mattered.

CHAPTER TWENTY-SIX

I had longed for the time I could explain to my children just how deeply in love their father and I grew. They had to have seen it all through the years of growing up within a cocoon of love and laughter that our simple lives were. They had to remember all the trips to the beach, parks, to most of the 'must see' monuments that made up the landscape of America. They had to remember the boyfriends and girlfriends and break ups and broken hearts we loved them through. Our lives had been rich with the most beautifully mundane day-to-day treasures that I just could not imagine they would turn their back on them. But, the truth may be that they could. This may have been shocking enough to turn them from me for good. Neither had been to see me since the day at my house. I thought of reaching back out to them, to force the issue but that would have once again proven Ruth right that I was and always had been selfish. So, I went about my days following the same routine. Morning coffee, help from Pam, activities in the group room, lunch with "the girls", afternoon nap, dinner in my room, then the night. The long nights with nothing to fill them except sadness and a heaviness of regret that was beginning to tax me physically, not just emotionally. And still I woke up every morning with a new hope for the day that I would hear from my children. I'm sure that is the work of God, His mercy is new every morning and the hope that goes along with it. As the sun sets in this beautiful adopted land I have grown to call home, that same hope dies. A change in the routine finally comes the morning I stay in bed. I was getting pretty old…maybe it was time to stop getting up so early…maybe a day in bed is just the thing to feel better…maybe two days is just the ticket. The new routine had begun.

"Ruth, hey it's Jon. Listen, I really think it's time for us to see her.

We agreed that no matter what, she raised us, loved us and was the only mother we knew. I got a call this morning from one of her nurses. It seems she hasn't been out of the bed in nearly two weeks. The nurse is afraid she has developed pneumonia and the doctor is seeing her today. I feel like we need to check on her. Then when she's up to it, we can find out the rest." Jon's speech was out before Ruth had time to say 'hello'.

"First of all, good morning Jon. Second of all, this is the weekend I spend with my grandchildren. And lastly, I don't know if I'm ready or not. I know I said we should, but I just don't know yet. You have always had a closer relationship with her. There has always been a struggle between us. I feel like I've forgiven her for so many of her short-comings that one more is just too much. And short-coming is hardly an adequate description! More like a lifetime of deceit! I know you feel like seeing her, so please, go ahead and see her. I just can't right now. If it will make you feel better, tell her… tell her I hope she feels better soon or something. Whatever, I'm just not going to be around her yet. Maybe in a few days, maybe in a few weeks."

"I'm stopping by there today. Hear what the doctor had to say. Do you want me to let you know?"

"Sure, whatever you want to do. Why don't you ask her how long it took her to come up with the elaborate story of our birth, of how Dad was so sure we were twins from the very beginning, not just one baby. See, I keep thinking of every detail that was a lie! This is exhausting. Go see her. Maybe you will feel better." Ruth shut and slid her phone across the breakfast table. Her husband looked over the top of his newspaper with a questioning look to which she shook her head. "I can't…I just can't."

Jon walked down the hall toward the noise of a busy nurses' station with nurses giving medications, taking off orders, admitting new residents… that beehive of activity he had seen many times over the past few years. He stopped by the nurses' station and waited for his mother's nurse to look up from her chart.

"Oh hey Jon. You just missed Dr. Stephens. Let me finish this one thing and I will come tell you what he said." Jon took the cue and walked on to his mother's room. He tapped on the wooden door and gently opened it in case she was sleeping. For just a moment he thought he had the wrong room. But that was definitely her room, her furniture and pictures. The woman lying there though was not his mother. The woman lying in his mother's bed was thin and frail, her hair was hanging down around her neck and shoulders with the stripe of grey turning into brown about one-third the way down. No, his mother would have never allowed that. No nice matching outfit, no jewelry, no make-up or red lipstick...whoever this lady was, she looked absolutely nothing like his mother. Just as he was about to rouse this stranger, the nurse tapped on the door and came in. She motioned for him to come to the door to talk more privately.

"Well, Dr. Stephens did say she has pneumonia, but after her blood work came back he said she had a mild heart attack as well. She has been lying in bed so much lately, pneumonia is less of a surprise than the heart attack. He has her on some blood thinner already. You may want to call him directly, but she's not doing very well right now. We have an order for IV antibiotics and another portable chest x-ray in three days. Now you know she's always been a spunky one, so she just might bounce right back from this. But just the same, you and Ruth might want to spend a little more time with her and talk to her. Do you have any questions for me?"

Jon shook his head in response. "You know how to reach Dr. Stephens so I'm going to see if the pharmacy has sent the antibiotics and get those started."

"Uh, yeah, ok you go ahead and I will give him a call. Thanks for calling me." Jon walked to the bedside and smoothed her hair back. She was pretty warm, a fever no doubt. Without all the fuss of her hair and make-up she looked fragile...like the soft thin tissue paper she always put around gifts. He reached behind him and pulled up the chair from her vanity.

"Hey mom. They are going to get you all fixed up, antibiotics and chest x-rays. Sorry I haven't been here to check on you. I didn't realize you were feeling so bad. I'm sure the nurses may have tried to call one of us. I've been gone for work and Ruth probably...well she probably didn't get the message. Now listen, you have to get better. We have a lot to talk about. I'm so sorry mom...I'm sorry about how we acted. I'm sorry you felt like you had to carry that burden all these years. It's going to be hard, but we can work through this. Ruth will be here too. Can you hear me mom?" Jon felt his throat starting to constrict as he tried to hold back the tears. He managed to get those words out without his voice cracking, but just barely. He didn't want her to think she was worse off than she was. But when he saw her like this…he felt so ashamed of how they had ignored her these past weeks. He felt ashamed for not coming to his senses sooner. After a lifetime with Effie as his mother, how could he have turned away from her like that? He hung his head and berated himself for his and his sister's behavior.

He stayed while the nurse started the IV. He talked to his mother and held her hand. She never flinched as the IV was started. He knew the sense of hearing was present even if a person wasn't responding so he continued to talk to her. The longer he talked to her, the less able he was to hold his tears at bay. She had to rally back from this. He had to know she heard his apologies and give him forgiveness. Jon immediately called Ruth as he pulled out of the parking lot. She was finally moved to feel some kind of softness toward her mother and regret for the past few weeks. But he wasn't sure if this would move her to see their mother.

I dreamed the most vivid dreams. I dreamed that I was sitting on a couch in a quirky little apartment. I dreamed that Emmerick was sitting next to me making small talk. I dreamed about my first kiss. So nice, such pleasant dreams. I dreamed of standing up with Dierk as he took me as his wife regardless of all that I had done and all that had been done to me. I dreamed of our nights together that made my first kiss pale in comparison. I dreamed of how it felt to love someone so completely you couldn't wait eight hours for them to get home from work. I dreamed of us growing old together. Such a blissful place to be. Back with the love of my life. Reaching out and feeling his hands that worked so hard to take care of me and the two children he inherited. Such a peaceful place to next to him, swinging on the porch swing watching a Southern sunset. I didn't want to stop dreaming. I didn't want them to turn into those nightmares.

I found myself looking around Lucy's empty apartment at the ransacked room, at the dresser drawers pulled out and emptied. I saw her pictures and perfume and make-up. I saw my hand reach out and take her lipstick off the dresser and I saw my hand pull out the picture and letter from her mirror. I wanted to wake up, this was always such a dreadful part. I could no more wait to read that letter than a child could wait to open Christmas presents. But this was no gift.

"Lucy! You know our time is running out! We have to get her out of here! It's getting too dangerous for her to be here. They will be rounding up more Jews any time now. Please help me Lucy! We have always been the best of friends and I need your help now. You said there was a girl you work with that might be able to help us. What do we need to do to convince her to help? You come up with a plan and I will go with it. Miriam doesn't have much time before the baby is born and I won't stand by and let anything happen to her! Lucy, she's the love of my life, I have to save her and our baby, no matter what happens to me. Meet me tonight at the café. Tell me your plan with this new girl. You're the only one I trust to help her! I will see you tonight.

Emmerick

How could they?? How could he? They were all in on it! All in on the grand plan to save Miriam and reunite her to Emmerick with their baby. I dreamed of the walk back home, of the walk to the barn, of the jealousy raging in my heart and the resentment that she was going to cost us our lives after all I had done for her. I dreamed of kneeling down next to her and hating her. She knew all along that I loved Emmerick! He knew! I dreamed of her constant noise and the car door. No! she would not cost me my life! She had to be quiet! I dreamed of my hand and hers joined to save our lives...did I do it? Did I kill her? In my heart I resented her...did I resent her enough to do this? I dreamed of the things she left her babies and of covering her face as we buried her. I fell on the fresh dirt and sobbed for her...for the loss of life...for the loss of their mother...for the regret of my part in it. I have to wake up! I've dreamed this too many times! I didn't kill her, Father said so!!

I jolted awake and found myself disoriented...in a room with furniture and a tube in my arm. I'm awake...I'm awake...I touched my face to feel that the sobbing had been real. Would I never know peace from that night? Would I never feel forgiveness for what had been in my heart? I had to have this punishment. But now...I'm so tired of carrying it. I want to feel the peace and the forgiveness. I took the children, I raised them as my own, and now they had to know the horrible truth. I will never see understanding in their eyes... never see forgiveness. I can pray for their peace though. I can pray they feel forgiveness in their hearts, not for my benefit, but for theirs.

Then the morning came, the morning that they showed up... Jon and Ruth. I could hear Ruth's high-pitched whisper and Jon's low tone response. I couldn't make out what they were saying, but I imagined Ruth protesting the visit and Jon coaxing her into it. I had to smile inwardly... they had held those same roles all of their lives.

Jon was the first to poke his head in the door. "Hey there Mom... up to some visitors?" He flashed that little boy smile. I pushed myself up in the bed as far as my decrepit limbs would push.

"Of course, I am! Always!!"

Ruth slipped in quietly behind him. Jon sat on the bed while Ruth leaned against the wall, barely inside the door.

I spoke first, "I'm so glad you both came! Are you two doing ok?"

"Well, I think the real question is are *you* doing ok? You've had quite a time with this pneumonia." Jon laid his hand gingerly on my leg.

"Oh, I'd say I'm going to come out of this battle the victor. Ruth, how are you?" I made a specific point to speak directly to my daughter.

Ruth looked down at her fidgeting hands, "I'm ok". Her voice cracked with just the two words. My heart went out to her.

"You certainly look better than you did the other day, Mom." Jon's attempt to keep the conversation progressing. "We were hoping you would feel like talking a little today. If you are up to it. We wanted to talk more about what you told us."

He looked at me expectantly, Ruth continued to discover the myriad of ways she could twist a Kleenex. I wanted to be an open book for my children. "Of course. Talk, ask questions, whatever you two want or need to know." I'm not sure if the noise that came from Ruth was a sniff or a snort of derision.

Jon glanced back at his sister then took the lead. "It was shocking to say the least. It was just so much to digest. I think I... we... feel lost at this point. We know our lives as a family were real, and nothing can replace our memories. I have so many questions, I'm at a loss where to begin. We can't begin to understand what all you went through Mom. But, I guess the burning question is why? Why did you keep this from us for so long? And why now?"

Ruth glanced up at her brother with a slight look of surprise on her face. She had not expected direct questioning from Jon right off the bat.

"Those are difficult questions to answer son, but worthy of the absolute truth. At first, when your father and I got married, it was a matter of safety for all of us. There was so much anti-Semitism you both could have been taken from us and we could have been imprisoned and killed for harboring you. After we moved to America, there were even prejudices here, though not nearly as severe so we continued to protect you. Back then, we were in the middle of the Cold War, there were still plenty of reasons to believe people still resented those of us who had helped the Jewish people. And I was always afraid. I was afraid there were some in Germany who were still looking for you two. Every reason we had was driven by fear. Once I returned home and realized I didn't have to fear as much as I did before, you two were already getting older, in elementary school and we were a normal family. And that was all I wanted. I wanted us to be a family, I wanted our home to be a safe place that we could create the lives we wanted and not just live in reaction to what had happened or what could happen. As for your second question, I have always felt like I stole you. And I felt like I robbed you of your heritage. The older I got, the more regrets I had. I don't know that there ever was a 'right time'. But I wanted you to know while I still had enough memory to tell you all the details and before I was gone and you would never know." That was the truth of it. Fear of telling them followed by fear of not telling them. Jon and Ruth were both looking down at their hands by this time. As always, Jon was the spokesperson.

"Mom… I can't even imagine the fear and torment you went through after all the life changing events you had to survive just to raise us as your own. I'm so very sorry…" Jon's own voice cracked as his words were silenced by a sudden choking sob. I reached out a wrinkled hand and put it on his that had never left my leg.

In a split-second Ruth had pushed away from the wall and was on her knees next to the bed. She grabbed the bed covers and buried her face in the blanket. Her body rocked and shook with the force of her cries. Her release was so much more than for the last few months. For years she had been at odds with me with absolutely no valid reason except she was inherently strong and felt she needed to be my exact opposite to be her own person. My heart was breaking for my two children… MY children. My throat was so constricted from trying to fight back the tears that I didn't dare speak. Instead, I gently laid my hand on her head. I could barely understand her when she began to speak into the blankets in between sobs and gasps of air.

"Mom… I'm so sor.. sor… sorry! I was so hard on you! And I don't know why! I didn't mean any of it Mom!" Ruth offered up the most cherished olive branch. I knew what a sacrifice it was for her to forgive me for a lifetime of lies. I didn't deserve it, but I had longed for it anyway.

We stayed in the position for just a while, Jon with his hand on my leg, Ruth with her head lying sideways on the bed and me with a hand on each one. We created a conduit for love… and forgiveness to flow. After a few more tears, more sniffles and many more tissues we knew it was time for them to leave.

"Mom, do you think you will feel like coming to the house Sunday? We are having brunch after church. Just us and you, if you feel like it." Jon and Ruth often ate together with their spouses on Sunday afternoons.

"Oh, I would love to. A day away from here and with my family is just the thing to get me completely over the last little remnants of this infection. I look forward to it!" I laid a hand on Ruth's cheek as they were saying goodbye. Those black eyes that were so much like Miriam's' that had haunted me for so long, only held love in them now.

CHAPTER TWENTY-SEVEN

Pam brushes and twists and pins as she has done for so many years. She has picked a very flattering skirt and sweater that match so nicely. She has always done such a wonderful job of matching clothes and fixing hair. Just before Jon and Ruth come in, Pam reaches in her pocket and pulls out the favorite tube of Montezuma Red lipstick and painstakingly applies it.

After the funeral, Jon and Ruth nod and thank a multitude of people for coming and for bringing food. They perform very well, they appear strong and respond to each person correctly. It takes hours for the well-wishers to visit, eat, and help clean up. Then it's just them. They walk through the house that they were raised in and wish one more time they could see her and talk to her. To tell her they understand and they love her not in spite of what she did but because of it.

"Jon...I can't even express my sorrow...I turned my back on her... and just when I thought we were going to be able to truly mend our relationship, she's gone and she will never know how I really felt!"

Jon and Ruth stood in the doorway of their mother's old room. Jon pulled Ruth into his chest and hugged her. "I believe she knew. I believe she always knew how we felt. You have to believe that too."

"How could she know? I never told her...I didn't know I could be so cold and heartless! Nobody could see love through that! How would she have known?"

"A mother just knows."

EPILOGUE

July 6, 1955

"Mom…mail ran! I'm getting it!"

"Ruthie, you be careful getting that mail! Watch the road!" That child is so head strong!

"Here mom, I'm going to play in the tree house."

Bills, advertisements, a letter for Dierk, and a letter for…me, but not my mother's handwriting.

Germany, 1950

"Hey. So, guess who I ran into today? You will never believe it! She was asking for you. Of course, I told her nothing…but now might be the time to track her down, before she leaves. I didn't ask anything about her. Anyway…I was very surprised. If you want to know what happened and if you ever want to see them, this might be your chance."

1955

Dearest Effie,

It has taken me a long time to find you! Please don't tear this up, please read it. I was so very happy to learn you made it through the war! I was also very sad that Miriam didn't. We all went through so much after that last day, I can't begin to tell you. I would love to see you again, talk to you, see for myself you have turned out well. If you want to reach me, I will be waiting. I won't try to come to you unless you ask. I'm sorry Effie, there is much I want to apologize for. I won't push. If you want to contact me, you have my address now. I hope you will.

Your friend from another life,
Lucy

Jon grabbed his glasses to check the clock as he also grabbed for his cell phone.

"Ruth? What is it? What's wrong?"

"Jon, I've been thinking…tossing and turning…I want to know. I want to know about our real parents. I want to know more about that time and place and what our mother went through and sacrificed for us. Will you help? Are you in?"

Jon placed a hand on his wife's arm to let her know this was not an emergency call. "Well, first of all our 'real' parents were Effie and Dierk Khol. Second, I'm not at all sure how we would begin, but if want to do this I'm in. So, what's your first thought, besides letting me go back to sleep?"

"Did you ever hear mom talk about someone named Lucy? Maybe she has the answers to the most important question, who was father and is he still alive? Whoever she is…I say we start there."